The World
Beyond The Gate

by
Sue Hoffmann

Best wishes.

Sue Hoffmann

Circaidy Gregory Press

Copyright Information

Acknowledgements

Special thanks once again to Kay Green of Circaidy Gregory Press for her encouragement and help. Her skilful editing has improved the story immeasurably, and her drawings for the chapter headings help to bring the tale to life. Thanks also to Katy Jones for her superb art work for the book cover and the troublesome 'fly-things', and to my good friend Kim Chapman for reading the first draft and helping me to sort out errors and confusions!

ISBN 978-1-910841-57-0

Printed in the UK
by Catford Print

Published September 2021
by Circaidy Gregory Press
Creative Media Centre, 45 Robertson St,
Hastings TN34 1HL

For Marian and Peggy

Chapter 1

A New Gate

Timothy dreamed he was back in Challenrah. The red-tinted grass was soft and springy beneath his bare feet. Nearby, Larn and the two other huge felines lay basking in the warmth of the orange sun, their long tails twitching gently. His friend Angela sat by them, stroking their reddish-green fur. Tim settled back against the slope of the hillside, happy to be here.

His peace was short-lived. A boy of about fifteen came racing up the hill to where he sat.

'Get up!' yelled the boy. 'Get up! It's all going wrong. Get up and help!'

A dark cloud covered the sun as Tim leapt to his feet. 'What's the matter?' he asked, but the boy didn't answer.

Something sharp pricked Tim's ankle. He looked down to see the grass turning brown and spiky. Rain began to fall, then hailstones that hurt as they hit his face. 'What's the matter?' he shouted through the suddenly strong wind. 'What's going on? Where's Devron?' but the boy and Angela had vanished from the hillside.

Tim cowered down as wind and hail battered against him. 'Angela?' he shouted. 'Devron?' The wind whipped his cries away.

Crouching on the soaking, dying grass, Tim felt the ground tremble as if it was in pain.

'Devron?' he called again, sure that the Gatekeeper who guarded the way between worlds would be able to help. 'Devron?'

Wetness coated his face, sticky and warm, as one of the great cats licked him.

'Get off, Larn,' he mumbled, shoving at the furry body pinning him down. The tongue slapped across his cheek again and he woke up.

He lay still for a moment, disoriented. 'Hi Jasper,' he said after a moment. The young dog whined and licked him even more vigorously. Tim ruffled the soft fur. 'Don't tell Mum you're on my bed again.' Pushing Jasper gently out of the way, he slid out of bed. 'Sorry I called you Larn. I was dreaming about Challenrah.'

Challenrah! The amazing land he'd found when he'd unlocked that old Gate in the pub garden back in England. He sat on the edge of the bed and put his arm around the dog. 'It was so real,' he told the young animal. 'It felt as though I was back there. Larn's a huge cat – sort of like a tiger but with big, pointed ears and reddish-green fur. And I'm sure it was Hamett shouting to me. He's Devron's nephew.' He stood up. 'Come on. We'll go for a walk.'

Jasper leapt off the bed and danced around Tim as he gathered up jeans and tee-shirt and headed to the bathroom for a hasty wash. Fifteen minutes later, he left a note for his mother and headed off to the Strand for Jasper's morning walk. It was one of Tim's favourite places in his new home in Oceanside, California.

Jasper tugged, trying to run ahead, while Tim ambled along taking little notice of his surroundings. Why had he dreamed about Challenrah? With all the excitement of the move to the States, starting at his new school and meeting Angela again, he'd managed not to think too much about the land through The Gate. Why dream about it now? And the dream had felt so real. It made him realise how much he still missed Challenrah. He missed Hamett and his sister Nashena. He missed Gatekeeper Devron and his wife Kallyn, and the Wardens. He didn't miss the shadows, though. He shivered at the memory of the creepy dark patches that had caused so much trouble in Tim's world and had threatened the safety of Challenrah. If he and Devron hadn't closed the wayward Gate permanently, those shadowy sprites would have slipped back through into Challenrah and all magic there would have been lost. What a price he'd had to pay for his decision to help Devron, though: he was shut out of that special land, with no way of knowing if he'd ever find a way back there.

Jasper's tug on the lead brought Tim back to the present. Surprisingly, the Strand walkway was deserted for once. 'Sorry, boy,' he said when Jasper barked, clearly wanting to chase some seagulls. 'You're not allowed off the lead on the Strand. It's "leash" here, isn't it? Are you listening, Jasper? Stop pulling. You're not allowed off the *leash*.' Jasper

3

pulled harder, keen to have a run, but Tim suddenly stood still, rooted to the spot.

A short way ahead, on a patch of concrete that led to some steps down to the beach, there was a gate. No fence, wall or hedge. Just a gate. Tim stared. That gate had not been there when he'd walked this way yesterday. He took one step closer and stopped again, half-expecting it to disappear.

Heart pounding, he made himself walk up to the gate. It was wooden, with five horizontal planks and one cross-piece, and a clear view of the Strand through the widely spaced planks. Two gateposts held the gate in place, one thicker than the other. A rusty chain was wrapped around the thicker post and an old padlock dangled at the bottom of the chain. With Jasper following closely, Tim walked twice around the gate. He ran his fingers over the rusty hinges that fixed it to the thick post. The chain on that post didn't seem to serve any purpose as far as Tim could see. It was draped round the gatepost but not the gate itself. He tugged at the chain and the padlock. They rattled but wouldn't come loose.

A latch on the top bar secured the gate to the thinner post. With shaking hands, Tim lifted the latch and pushed at the gate. It swung open and Jasper yanked him through the gap. Tim stepped forward, expecting – hoping – to see the landscape change from Strand to red-tinted grass. What time of day would it be in Challenrah? Would Devron be there to meet him, along with Larn and the other two great cats that trailed the Gatekeeper almost everywhere?

Standing on the other side of the gate, Tim stared at the view ahead. Disappointment hit him like a cold shower. He was still on the Strand, not in Challenrah. He wiped his sleeve across damp eyes.

'What did I think would happen?' he asked as Jasper stared up at him. 'It's just a gate.'

But it couldn't be "just a gate"; he was sure of that. First the awful dream, and now finding this gate. It couldn't be coincidence. What if he was needed in Challenrah and the gate had appeared so that he could get there? The more he considered the idea, the more obvious it seemed. Something was wrong – again – in Challenrah and he had to get back there. Opening the latch hadn't worked but there must be some way to cross into Devron's world.

'A key,' Tim said aloud. 'It must need a key. Look at the padlock, Jasper. If I open that, maybe the gate'll open properly – into Challenrah. Bet there's one here somewhere, just waiting for me to find it.'

Towing a reluctant Jasper, Tim searched the area around the new gate.

'Nothing there,' he informed the uninterested dog. 'That's odd. Wait, though! I kept the old key: the one that opened The Gate in *The Grey Lady* pub garden. What if that's the key we need? It must be. Come on. I have to get that key.'

Unimpressed, the dog merely sniffed at the grassy patches around the gateposts. Desperate to go home and get the key, Tim closed the gate and set off at a jog with Jasper at his heels.

Angela ran across the grass of the dog park and skidded to a halt by Tim. 'Got your text,' she said. 'You know I'm always up early on a Saturday. Why didn't you text this morning? And why didn't we meet at the new Gate?'

'It's got a padlock,' Tim said.

'And?'

'Can't find the key,' Tim mumbled.

'What d'you mean, you can't find the key? You have to find it!'

'I know that,' Tim snapped back. 'There wasn't one by The Gate. The new Gate, I mean.' He'd started calling it *The Gate* now, as if, like The Gate back in England that had led him into Challenrah, it needed capital letters. 'I think we need the old key and I can't find it. That's what I spent the morning doing: looking for it.' He slumped down onto the grass.

Angela sat next to him and stroked Jasper. 'You put it in a safe place, didn't you?'

Tim glared at her. 'It's not there.'

'We've waited months,' Angela said. 'A Gate's here and you've lost the key. Great job, Tim. Are you sure you looked properly by the new Gate?'

'Course I did. Nothing there.'

'But–'

'I looked, Angela! Last time, with the old Gate, I found the key straight away. That key must be the one we need. I know I kept it.'

'We have to get back to Challenrah,' Angela said. 'Your dream must mean we're needed.'

Jasper's tail thudded against the grass.

'Where's Challenrah?'

Angela and Tim stared at the girl standing near them.

'Hi Madison,' said Angela. 'Didn't hear you coming.'

'Jasper did,' Madison pointed out. She dropped her backpack onto the ground and sat down.

Tim opened his mouth to tell her to go away, and shut it again without saying anything. Madison was a bit of a nuisance, always following Angela about, but Tim remembered what it was like to be bullied and left out of things. He didn't want to make her feel rejected, even if he resented her at times. How had she found them out here in the dog park anyway? Was it just by chance?

'Where's Challenrah?' Madison repeated. She rummaged in her pack, took out her drawing pad and a pencil and started to sketch Jasper.

'Nowhere,' Tim lied. 'It's... er... It's a codename we made up for the project we've chosen for Miss Wilson. Have you started yours?'

Madison looked up from her drawing. 'No. Can I join in with you?'

Tim frowned. How many times had lies got him into trouble at home and in Challenrah? And here he was, lying once more. 'Well...' he began, and broke off to swat at a huge fly hovering above his nose. Jasper gave a low growl. The fly moved away then came straight back. Tim swiped at it again.

Angela thumped him on the arm. 'What are you doing?'

'That fly's driving me nuts,' he muttered, waving his hand in front of his face. Jasper growled again.

Angela peered at him. 'What fly?'

'That one.' Tim pointed. 'It's enormous. What kind is it, Madison?'

'What fly?' Madison asked.

Tim's temper flared. 'Don't pretend you can't see it! It's– Oh. It's gone.'

Angela and Madison started to laugh but Tim wasn't amused. The thing had been big, mean-looking and all-too-real. Its body was dark and its wings were grey. It had at least ten long, floaty legs. Ten legs? Insects had six legs, not ten. Grey wings and dark body? Like a shadow? Tim shuddered as memories of the *raffakins* came flooding back; *raffakins*: the mischievous, shadowy sprites from Challenrah that had become truly evil in Tim's world. Was this nasty-looking fly like those shadows? Had it escaped from Challenrah through the new Gate, or been sent through?

'Can I?' Madison asked again.

Tim stared at her. 'Can you what?'

'Join in with your project?'

Tim shook his head. 'Miss Wilson said we had to work in pairs.'

'No,' Madison argued. 'She said pairs or groups of three.'

Angela nudged Tim. 'Let her join in. Her drawings are great. We'll have the best illustrations in the class.'

'I'll think about it,' Tim said. He stood up and tugged at Angela's sleeve. 'We have to go. Bye, Madison. See you at school on Monday. We'll sort out the project thing then.'

Before either girl could object, he pulled Angela to her feet and headed off, hauling her with him. Jasper trotted after them.

'Hey,' Angela protested.

'Come on!' Tim urged. 'We have to find a way back to Challenrah. There's something really bad going on. I know there is.'

'You might be right,' Angela retorted. 'And maybe we *could* get back – if you hadn't lost the key!'

Chapter 2

Challenrah

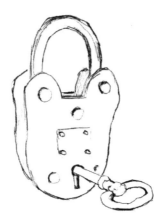

'What a mess, Tim!'

Tim spun round guiltily. Peter, his step-dad, was standing in the bedroom doorway with Cassie in his arms. Tim hastily gathered up the clothes and boxes that were strewn around the floor. 'Having a sort-out,' he said.

'Oh. Well. Good for you. Don't be long. Dinner's almost ready. Your Mum's going to be late so it's just the three of us. Are you okay to look after your sister while I finish cooking?'

Cassie stuck her finger in her mouth. 'Down,' she said around the finger, and Peter set her on the carpet next to Tim.

Tim spread everything out again as Peter walked away. 'He might have waited for an answer,' he said to Cassie, handing her a comic. 'Here. Look at the pictures. I'm busy.'

He returned to his search. The key had to be here somewhere. He'd found the small box where he'd put the key and the Gatekeeper badge that Devron had given him after he'd agreed to help with the old, faulty Gate. The badge was there, along with the disc-shaped pendant that allowed him to look like a Challendrian, but where was the key? He remembered putting the box on the shelf at the top of the built-in wardrobe. He'd shoved some other boxes up there too, containing a few toys he'd brought from England and some books and comics he wanted to keep. They'd fallen down a couple of times until he'd stacked them properly. Could the key have dropped out? Why had he never bothered to check?

Jasper grabbed one of Tim's trainers from the bottom of the wardrobe and ran round the bedroom with it, daring Tim to chase him. Usually up for a game, this time Tim was too distracted.

'Drop it, Jasper!' he ordered crossly. Jasper dropped the trainer next to Cassie and slunk into the corner of the room.

Immediately contrite, Tim went over to the young dog. The people at the animal shelter had explained how Jasper had been shouted at and hit in his last home. They'd warned that he was frightened of loud voices. 'I want this one,' Tim had said when his mother had suggested a different dog. 'He's been bullied. He needs a good home.'

Tim put his arm around the trembling dog. 'Sorry, Jasper,' he said. 'You've settled in really well, you know. You're much more confident than when we first got you.'

Beneath his gentle hands, Jasper began to relax. More memories came back: placing his hands on Devron to heal him when the Gatekeeper had been injured; helping to cure Hamett's head injury; using his Gift of healing to help Devron close the sick Gate.

'My Gift was strong in Challenrah,' he told Jasper. 'It's never worked here before but I think maybe it's working a bit now, don't you? You've stopped shaking. Good boy. You know, I bet whatever talents I had in Challenrah would strengthen if I could get back there. Cassie, what're you doing? That's my trainer. It won't fit you. Give it here.'

Cassie giggled and went on trying to pull the trainer over her shoe. Tim laughed.

'Come on,' he said, 'let's go downstairs before your daddy calls us. I'll finish this later.'

Cassie held up the trainer and shook it. The key fell out onto the carpet.

'The key! The key!' Tim shouted, dancing around the bedroom. He snatched it up before Jasper could take it, then lifted Cassie and swung her round until she squealed with delight.

'More!' she demanded when he put her down.

'More later,' he told her. 'Come on, Key-Finder-Extraordinary. Let's go and eat.'

Tim gobbled his dinner rather too quickly. He burped loudly. 'Sorry,' he said before Peter could tell him off for bolting his food. 'Must have been hungry. Can I take Jasper out now?'

'It's "May I?"' Peter corrected. 'And yes, you may go – but be back by eight-thirty. Have you got your phone?'

'Yes,' Tim said, jumping up from the table. He grabbed Jasper's leash and ran out of the house with the dog hot on his heels.

He phoned Angela as he headed along the Strand. 'I've found the key,' he said. 'Meet me by The Gate.'

He'd hoped the area around The Gate would be deserted again but a number of people were out along the Strand, enjoying the warm, Saturday evening. Trying to appear casual, he sat down with his back against the gatepost wrapped with the chain. Jasper plonked himself down at Tim's feet. The fifteen-minute wait before Angela arrived seemed an eternity.

'You took your time,' Tim complained.

'Your directions weren't too hot,' Angela retorted. She studied The Gate. 'It doesn't look like the old Gate.'

'It's still a *Gate*, though,' Tim said. 'I'm sure it is. Remember when you joined my class just before the end of term last year? You knew all about Challenrah already. We had some amazing times there, didn't we?'

'Get on with it, Tim,' Angela instructed.

Tim stared at her. 'What?'

'The key. Have you tried the key?'

'With all these people around? How could I?'

'What people?' Angela said.

Tim blinked hard. 'There were lots of them.'

'Well they're not here now,' Angela pointed out. She lifted the cord at her neck to show the disc-shaped pendant she was wearing. 'Did you remember your pendant?'

Tim nodded. 'I'm wearing it.' He had the Gatekeeper badge tucked safely away in his pocket but he didn't mention that.

13

Angela pointed to the padlock. 'Go on, then.'

Tim knelt on the grassy patch at the foot of the gatepost. 'What if it doesn't fit?' he asked.

'Just try it,' Angela said impatiently.

Tim looped Jasper's leash around his left wrist. With hands that refused to stay steady, he fumbled with the padlock and key. To his utter astonishment, the key slid in and turned easily. Carefully, he lifted away the padlock.

'Should I take the chain off?' he asked.

Angela shook her head. 'Someone might notice. We can always do that if The Gate doesn't open.'

Tim stood up. 'Go on then. Unlatch it.'

'You do it.'

'Why me?'

Angela shrugged. 'You found The Gate.'

Tim unlatched The Gate, opened it just a fraction and then paused. 'What if it won't take us to Challenrah?'

'You'll never know till you try it, will you?' said Madison.

Madison? What was she doing here?

Before Tim had the chance to ask her, Jasper took off through the narrow gap between the open Gate and the gatepost. Still with the leash around his wrist, Tim was yanked through, barging The Gate fully open as he crashed past. Jasper raced forward, dragging Tim along so fast that he lost his balance. The leash was dragged out of his hand as he sprawled full length on the ground. He lay there, wondering if he was hurt or just winded. Had he landed on concrete or on the grass of Challenrah? As his breath returned, he knelt upright and looked around.

Red-tinted grass. Orange sun. Challenrah! He was back where he'd longed to be.

Cushioning, springy grass had saved him from any serious injury but his right hand was hurting. Glancing down, he noticed he was still clutching the padlock with the key in it. His fall had jammed the metal into his palm, bruising him but, fortunately, not cutting the skin. He stuffed the lock and key into his pocket, stood up and rubbed his sore hand against his jeans.

The Gate was closed and Jasper was sniffing around the gateposts. There was no sign of Angela and Madison, nor of anyone else. Where were the Wardens? There should have been Wardens or a Gatekeeper guarding the new way between worlds.

Certain that Angela would be following as soon as she could, Tim sat down by The Gate to wait for her. Madison was a complication. What was she doing there anyway? Angela would have to bring her or think up an explanation for why Tim had apparently disappeared from the Strand. It was strange that Angela wasn't already here, though. She'd been right behind him when Jasper tugged him through.

It was good to be back but Tim's stomach refused to let him relax. It kept churning uncomfortably and Tim knew it was from anxiety rather than his rushed meal. In his dream, Hamett had dashed up the hill, shouting that something was wrong, and then the grass had turned brown and spiky. As far as Tim could tell, the grass around The Gate was normal enough for Challenrah. It was soft and bouncy – and it had protected him when he'd fallen. Everything looked fine.

He was relieved to see that the orange sun was just rising. Time stood still back home while there was daylight in Challenrah. He had hours before he needed to think about getting back, but checking whether or not he could open The Gate from this side seemed a good idea. Last time he'd been in Challenrah, he'd needed either special powder or Devron's help to open the old Gate in order to return home. He studied the back of this new Gate a bit more carefully. It was a mirror image of the one on the Strand, with a padlock on a chain that looped around the thicker gatepost. The padlock was shut and his key wouldn't fit. He was stuck – but he'd face that problem later. Right now, he was beginning to worry about being so alone out here.

The sound of a burbling stream nearby told him he was not on the steep hillside he was used to. He knew a Gateway from Challenrah could form anywhere it chose but he'd half-expected this new Gate to open up where the other one had been. The stream looked clear enough, rippling over yellow, grey and brown pebbles and with a few tiny, silvery fish darting through the water, but the reeds along the bank were dry and withered, reminding him of the dying grass in his dream.

'What now, Jasper?' he asked. 'We can't just wait around. Don't know exactly where we are but I have a feeling the old Gate used to be somewhere near here, so we can't be too far from Devron's village. Which way do I go to get there?'

Jasper made the decision for him. The young dog came bounding through the long grass and skidded to a halt against Tim's legs, almost knocking him into the stream. Tim tried to grab the end of the leash but Jasper darted away and Tim jogged after him. Leash trailing, Jasper slowed to a steady trot, turning back now and again to check that Tim was following. Tim's watch had stopped working – as always happened in Challenrah – but he reckoned he'd been chasing after Jasper for about ten minutes before he came within sight of some cottages. The nearer he approached, the more certain he became that this was indeed Devron's village. He had come to it from a completely different angle but, now he was here, he could see in the distance the hill where the old Gate had stood.

Jasper ran back to him, and he snatched up the leash while he had the chance. He wanted Jasper close to him for the dog's own safety in case Devron's felines were around. He hadn't seen any dogs in Challenrah on his previous visits so had no idea how Larn, Syeesha and Parrin would react to Jasper.

Excited and nervous at the same time, Tim walked through the village. It was strangely quiet. There were no market stalls, but that wasn't what troubled him. Even when it wasn't a Market Day, there should have been more people around, shopping at the few permanent small stores. The place was ominously quiet. It should be packed with people, bustling and noisy, like the Sunset Market held in Oceanside every Thursday evening. Tim's mouth watered at the memory of the fantastic variety of food stalls in the Sunset Market. There had been food stalls in this market square too, once, but now the place looked shabby and neglected.

He jumped as a couple of women passed close by, and then a man carrying a basket with a few loaves in it.

'No one's taking any notice of us, Jasper,' he said. 'Looks as if my pendant's doing its job.' Jasper looked up and wagged his tail. 'Must be sending the magic down the leash to make you look Challendrian, too. Nobody's given you a second glance, have they?'

With growing concern, he left the main market area behind and headed for the row of cottages he knew best, coming at last to a halt by the house that had belonged to Devron, his wife Kallyn and their nephew and niece, Hamett and Nashena.

Tim recalled how terrified he'd been on the day Devron's home had been destroyed by fire. He gripped Jasper's leash harder and stared at a cottage that looked just as it had when he'd first seen it. There was no sign of any fire-damage.

Time's different here, Angela had once told him. Tim swallowed hard and wiped suddenly sweaty hands down his jeans. How different could it be after he'd been away for almost a year? Would it have moved on – or had he gone back to a time before the old Gate had failed?

Chapter 3

A Talent for Healing

Tim walked down the short path and knocked on the front door. There was no answer. With Jasper in tow, he went down the side of the cottage. The small gate that led into Devron's back garden was open and he went straight in. The garden was almost as he remembered, with trees providing shade in one corner, but there were only a few straggly flowers in what had been well-tended borders.

There was a girl of about his own age sitting in the shade, leaning against one of the trees. She stood up as Tim entered the garden.

'Timoth!' she cried, running to him and flinging her arms around him. 'I knew you'd come.'

Embarrassed and bewildered, Tim bore the hug for a moment before gently pushing her away. It was strange to hear his Challendrian name of Timoth – particularly since it came from a girl he didn't recognise. Jasper had no such reservations. Tail waving madly, he jumped up at the girl, pestering until she knelt down and stroked him.

'It's lovely' she said. 'What is it?'

'A dog,' Tim replied. 'His name's Jasper.'

With the girl occupied with Jasper, Tim had the chance to look at her more closely. Her olive skin and amber eyes were normal for Challendrians, as were her loose, light-coloured trousers and tunic. He didn't think he'd met her before and yet there was something very familiar about her.

She glanced up at him and realisation hit him like a slap in the face. 'Nashena?'

The girl smiled. 'Took you long enough to work it out.' She moved back into the shade and Jasper lay down by her with his head on her lap.

Tim suppressed a twinge of jealousy and stopped himself from calling Jasper back. It was good that the young dog was confident enough to be friendly with other people. 'Last time I saw you, you were five years old,' he said. At least he knew now that time had moved on and not back.

'Five and a half,' corrected Nashena. 'It's been six years since you were here. It's been a long wait.'

Tim frowned. 'What? You haven't been waiting for me all that time? You can't have been.'

'Course not,' Nashena said, 'but since Devron sensed you at The Gate, I've been coming here every day – for the past two weeks.'

'Sensed me? Devron knew I was coming?'

Nashena nodded. 'He felt the new Gateway to your world forming. He said it would appear somewhere near you, and that you'd find it.'

20

'Well it did, and I did,' said Tim. 'I thought Devron could communicate with me telepathically since I said he could – just before we closed the old Gate. If he called me, I didn't hear him.'

'I don't think he did call you, but something's brought you back here. Anyway, we've more important things going on than your communication problems.'

Tim sat down by her and Jasper shifted across the grass to lean against Tim's knee. He put his arm around the dog. 'It's really odd. I remember you as a little child and now you're nearly my age. What's going on? Where is everyone? When was the cottage rebuilt? Does Devron need help with the new Gate?'

Nashena chuckled. 'Hamett said you always did ask a lot of questions.'

'Yeah, well, people have a habit of not telling me anything unless I ask. Where's Devron?'

'He's checking The Gate.'

'No, he's not. No one was there when I came through.'

'Not that Gate,' Nashena said. 'The other one.'

'What other one? What's going on? Why wasn't anyone guarding *my* Gate?'

Nashena glanced up at the gathering clouds. 'Wonder if it's going to rain? We could do with some rain. The ground's really dry.'

'I don't care about the weather,' Tim snapped. 'I need some answers. And I'm worried about Angela. She was called Anaga here, remember? She was just behind me when I came through The Gate. I don't know where she is.' He didn't mention Madison. With any luck, she'd been left behind.

Nashena tilted her head to one side as if listening for something. 'She's not far away,' she said after a moment. 'She's with—'

'A Warden?' Tim interrupted hopefully.

'Yes. Two of them – and someone else from your world.'

Tim muttered something impolite.

'What?'

'Nothing. Doesn't matter.' At least Angela was safely through into Challenrah. 'How d'you know they're coming? Have you started to get powers like the Wardens? Tell me about this other Gate.'

'I'll tell you on the way,' Nashena said.

Something buzzed past Tim's face. He jerked back. 'Wow! What was that?' He stood up to try to see the creature that had flown so close to him. It had been moving fast but he was almost certain it was a thing with long, dangly legs – like the one he'd seen in the dog park.

Nashena wasn't taking any notice of him. She lifted a pack that had been on the ground beside her and hoisted it over her shoulder. 'Come on, Timoth.'

Tim took a firm hold of Jasper's leash and followed her out of the garden. 'There weren't many people about in the village,' he said. 'Where is everyone?'

'Mostly out working in the fields,' Nashena replied. 'They're trying to sow more crops. Some have left, though. They've moved to Dallaharrin.'

'Where's that?'

22

'It's a village about a five-day walk from here.'

'Why have they left?'

'Look around, Timoth,' said Nashena. 'Didn't you see the fields as you came here? The harvest was poor last year and failed completely this year. We don't know why.'

'And this Dalliharn place is all right?'

'Dallaharrin,' Nashena corrected him. 'It's better than here – for now, anyway. We're having to bring food in from villages that still have some to spare.'

'Is that where you're taking me? Dallaharrin? I can't, Nashena. It's too far. I have to be back through The Gate before it's dark.'

'I know. Time will only stay still for you in your world while it's daylight here. Don't worry; we're only going to meet the Wardens. It's Jeznia and Carradin with Anaga.'

Tim remembered the two Senior Wardens. Jeznia was small and quietly spoken, but she had an air of authority about her. As for Carradin – the impressive scar that ran in a thin line from his right eye to his chin had always fascinated Tim. He still wanted to know how Carradin had come by that scar.

Don't worry, Nashena had said. The crops had failed; Angela hadn't come through The Gate with him but she was here now; Madison was in Challenrah; Devron wasn't around to sort everything out. What could be more worrying than all of that?

Questions burned in Tim's mind but the sight of the almost deserted village stopped him from speaking as they walked along. He was thankful when they left the main street behind and came to the edge of the village.

'There they are,' Nashena said, pointing ahead.

Tim smiled when he saw Angela. He ignored Madison. How had she managed to enter Challenrah? It was his land, wasn't it? His and Angela's. Well, Devron's and the Challendrians really, but he and Angela belonged here too, didn't they? Madison was an intruder. Why couldn't she have stayed behind, along with that backpack and sketch pad she always carried around?

He had no chance to ask Angela what had happened at The Gate. Carradin was supporting Jeznia, almost carrying her, and Tim could see as they approached how pale she was.

'Come here, Timoth,' Carradin ordered, setting Jeznia down carefully on the thick trunk of a fallen tree.

Great, thought Tim. *Here we go again. No greeting. No explanations. Just orders. Why did I bother coming back?*

'Hurry, lad,' said Carradin. 'She's been stung. Don't know what did it, but she's in a bad way.'

'What am I supposed...' Tim began, and stopped. He knew what he was supposed to do. He'd healed Devron – twice – and Hamett during his previous visits to Challenrah. He needed to help Jeznia now.

Jeznia managed a weak smile as Tim sat by her. 'My arm,' she said, pushing back the sleeve of her tunic.

Tim gulped. The whole of the Warden's forearm was red and blotchy, and there were several huge, yellow blisters just above her wrist. Carradin and the others were watching him expectantly but Tim didn't want to touch Jeznia's arm.

24

Madison stepped closer. 'Angela said you're a healer in this world. Doesn't look to me as if you know what you're doing.'

Tim glared at her. 'Who asked you to interfere? What would you know, anyway?'

He looked again at Jeznia's arm. He had to try, not only to help Jeznia but to prove Madison wrong. If he covered the blisters and blotches with her sleeve... There. Now the inflammation was hidden he could bear to rest his hand on the Warden's arm. She flinched as he touched her but nodded for him to carry on. He closed his eyes and sought out the root of the problem. A small lump part-way down her forearm was the source of the infection. He could feel heat there and could sense the spreading toxin.

Work slowly, Devron had told him, and Tim tried to control the urge to blast away the contamination. He sensed the response as the heat lessened beneath his fingers but something was wrong. However hard he concentrated, he could not rid Jeznia of all the inflammation and swelling.

Suddenly tiring, he leaned back and watched as Jeznia rolled up her sleeve. There was a definite improvement – the redness had faded and the blotches were gone – but the blisters remained.

'Well done,' Jeznia said, although Tim was disappointed with the results. 'It's much less sore and the dizziness has gone. Thank you, Timoth.'

'Good to see some colour back in your face, Senior Warden Jeznia,' Carradin said. His tone was light but he'd obviously been extremely concerned. He patted Tim on the shoulder. 'Glad to have you back, son. Just in time, too.'

Tim wanted to protest that it wasn't his fault he'd been kept out of Challenrah. He'd come back as soon as he'd found the new Gate. 'I'll try again later,' he told Jeznia.

'I'd appreciate that,' she said, 'but for now, I can manage. Thank you again.'

'That's all right,' Tim said, standing up and looking straight at Madison. 'I'm glad I could help.' He turned to Carradin. 'All Gatekeepers have healing talents, don't they?'

Carradin nodded. 'They do, although the strength of that Gift varies.'

'Well, I've only just thought about it, but when I first came through the old Gate and had to heal Devron...'

'After those rebels had put an arrow in his shoulder. Yes. Go on.'

'Why didn't another Gatekeeper help him?'

'No one available then, Timoth,' Carradin answered. 'There were only two other Gatekeepers at that time, and both were some distance away, guarding newly arrived Gates that couldn't be left untended. You were badly needed.'

Jeznia stood up a little unsteadily. 'I'm feeling better,' she said. 'Let's move on. I want Timoth to see the fields by the old barn.'

'What's going on?' Tim asked, but Nashena held up her hand, stood listening for a moment and then said, 'Devron's coming.'

Chapter 4

Devron

They were just specks in the distance at first, moving swiftly and kicking up a cloud of dust that made it hard to see any individuals. The noise grew as they drew closer – a steady drumming that reverberated through the ground and set Tim's teeth on edge. He was smugly pleased to note that Madison looked petrified.

They were nearer now and Tim stared open-mouthed at the sight of Devron riding a huge, horse-like creature, with the three large felines keeping pace alongside. They were approaching very fast.

'They're not going to stop in time,' Tim muttered.

They did, though. Just metres away from the Wardens and the children, Devron reined in the horse-thing and it skidded to a halt, raising yet more dust from the dry ground. The great cats slithered to a stop, sneezing in the dust. Jasper yelped and hid behind Tim. Devron swung his leg over the horse-thing's neck and slid down.

Tim opened his mouth to greet the Gatekeeper but found himself flat on his back with a great weight on his chest. 'Get off, Larn,' he begged. 'Can't breathe! You're squashing me.' The feline planted a sloppy lick across Tim's face. 'Oof!' said Tim as Larn's enormous paw landed on his stomach. 'Get off me!' The feline licked him again before clambering off him.

Tim stood up and rubbed his stomach. Larn leaned his head against Tim's side and Tim tickled the pointed, tufted ears. 'Glad to see you, too, Larn,' he said, secretly pleased that the big cat had remembered him. 'Just stop landing on me.' He spun round. 'Where's Jasper?' He couldn't see the dog. Had he run off, frightened by all the commotion?

'He's here,' said Madison, and Tim saw that she was holding the leash and comforting the trembling animal. They looked as terrified as each other.

Angela had run to Devron, and the Gatekeeper was walking towards Tim and the Wardens, his arm around Angela's shoulders. Devron nodded towards Tim. *I'll speak with you in a moment.*

Tim blinked in surprise. Devron hadn't spoken aloud yet Tim had heard his voice quite clearly. He'd forgotten the strange feeling of having someone speak in your head.

While Devron talked with the Wardens, Tim had time to study the horse-thing. It was taller and had longer legs than a normal horse, and it had a slightly longer neck, too. Its head looked pretty horse-like – perhaps narrower around the muzzle, and the tips of its ears were folded down – but its feet were more like those of a camel. A straggly mane flopped over one side of its neck. It snorted, twitched its long, thick tail and shook dust off its shaggy fur, revealing a reddish-grey coat. There was a rope bridle, but no saddle. Some bags were draped across its broad back.

Larn padded back to Syeesha and Parrin, and the three cats loped off into the long grass. Jasper whined and tugged Madison towards Tim.

'Thanks,' he said as he took hold of the leash. At least the felines hadn't paid any attention to Jasper. Maybe he could introduce the dog to Larn a bit later, as long as Jasper wasn't too scared. Larn was fully-grown now and even bigger than his dad Parrin.

'What's going on?' Madison asked.

'No idea,' Tim said unhelpfully.

'I guess you don't like me very much, do you?' Madison said. 'Is it because I'm black?'

Tim's eyes widened in shock at the question. 'What? No. Course not. My best friend back in England was black. We still Skype each other.'

'What is it then?'

'Nothing,' Tim said. 'Just shut up a minute, will you?'

He dragged a reluctant Jasper a bit nearer to the fallen tree where Jeznia was sitting down again, with Devron next to her. The Gatekeeper had his hand on the Warden's bad arm.

Carradin had once told Tim that Devron was probably the finest healer on Challenrah. Tim was sure the Gatekeeper would be able to cure Jeznia, but Devron looked concerned.

This isn't easy to heal, the Gatekeeper said to Tim.

'I know,' Tim said aloud.

Devron glanced round at him and smiled. *Try it my way,* he suggested.

Tim concentrated hard, thinking out each word separately. *I... got... rid... of...*

The Gatekeeper chuckled and Tim went red. 'I'm trying,' he said.

Just direct the speech at me in your mind, Devron instructed, *and "say" the words normally, as if you're talking to me.*

'Right.' *I got rid of some of the inflammation but the rest wouldn't go. I don't think it was just because I'm still quite new at this.*

The words had come out in a rush, but Devron nodded his understanding. 'Young Timoth's done a fine job here,' he said aloud, and Tim basked in the praise. So, it wasn't his fault that he couldn't heal Jeznia completely. 'I've cleared the blisters, Jeznia,' Devron went on, 'but there's still some infection under the site of the sting, and that's odd. What stung you?'

Jeznia shook her head. 'I didn't see it. I was down by the stream, checking those rushes that are dying, and I felt the sting.'

Devron patted her shoulder. 'No matter. We'll keep a check on that arm to make sure it doesn't flare up again. Let me – or Timoth – know immediately if it starts causing you any pain.'

Tim couldn't help himself. He looked across at Madison and grinned. She scowled back.

'How's The Gate, Devron?' Carradin asked.

'Which one?'

'Both, I suppose, although I meant the one Vallend's supposed to be looking after.'

Devron nodded. 'Vallend's Gate's still a problem but Timoth's new Gate is stable. I've asked Evrald and his team to keep a check on it because it's new, but it shouldn't cause any difficulty. It settled as soon as Timoth came through.'

Tim swelled with pride. *His* Gate, and it was fine because he'd passed through it. Let Madison chew on that for a while!

Devron had mentioned Evrald, and Tim recalled first meeting him, along with Carradin, Jeznia and Kallyn, on one of his visits to Devron's cottage. Tim knew that three Senior Wardens could control a Gate for a while if no Gatekeeper was available. His Gate would be in good hands. This other Gate, though... Presumably Vallend was a Gatekeeper, like Devron, so why should Devron be involved?

'And Vallend's Gate?' Carradin prompted. 'He's qualified and capable. Why did he call you in?'

Tim shuffled a bit nearer, unashamedly eavesdropping. Devron had once told him he'd make a good Gatekeeper, so he had a right to know about these Gates, didn't he?

'He didn't call me in,' Devron said. 'That Gate's been unpredictable since it formed, hasn't it? It shifted again and I sensed Vallend was having difficulty keeping it closed.'

'Where were his Wardens?' Carradin asked. 'They should have been there to help, shouldn't they?'

'Vallend tells me there've been more problems with the vegetation and the crops around his village. He'd sent them to investigate.'

'Leaving him with an unreliable Gate?'

Devron shrugged. 'He's skilled. He thought he could cope.'

'You've sorted it?'

'For the present. Kallyn's stayed to help until I get back there.'

'Why don't you close it permanently?' Tim asked. The old Gate in the pub garden had been faulty – due to sabotage by a group of rebels – and he'd had to help Devron shut it permanently in order to stop the nasty, shadowy *raffakins* from creeping back into Challenrah and harming the land. The Gate and the Gateway between Tim's world and Challenrah had disappeared once The Gate was double-locked, leaving Tim and Angela unable to return to Challenrah, until now. If Devron locked this other Gate that was causing trouble then it, too, would disappear. Problem solved.

Carradin glared at him and Tim looked down at the ground. Perhaps he shouldn't have interrupted the adults. 'Sorry,' he began, 'but I thought…'

'It's all right, Timoth,' Devron said. 'Each Gate is different. Some have to be locked on both sides to close them permanently – like the old Gate you locked for me. Others need their latch or a bolt removed just on our side. Sometimes Gates form and then disappear almost straight away, but until a Gate that has settled here is ready to leave of its own accord, it never wants to be shut permanently so it's always tricky to find a way to make that happen if something goes wrong and we have to intervene. Normally, we have no need to close a Gate permanently before it's ready to go.'

'Has this Gate that Vallend's looking after settled here?'

Devron nodded. 'Yes, but it's unstable and possibly dangerous. We're working on a way to either stabilise it or shut it down.'

'How long has it been here?' Tim asked.

'It appeared just over two years ago,' Devron said. 'It opened briefly but Vallend shut it almost immediately. Then it started to shift position very slightly, sometimes each day and sometimes after a week or more. The movement's barely detectable but we have to be very careful when we go near to a Gate that won't stay still.'

Was this why he'd been drawn back to Challenrah? Tim wondered. Was he supposed to help find a way to control this Gate? He was about to ask Devron this when Carradin spoke.

'You could have stayed there longer,' Carradin said. 'We'd have sent you our reports.'

Devron's face lit with a smile. 'I wanted to see Anaga and Timoth. It may not have been long for you youngsters, but it's been six years for us. I'm sorry I wasn't there to greet you when you came through the new Gate.' He turned to Madison. 'And I need to find out all about you, young lady. Why did Timoth's Gate let you through, I wonder?'

'It let me through, too,' Angela pointed out. 'I always had to have help before.'

'It knew you'd been here previously,' Devron told her, 'and you came through at the same time as Timoth. It recognised his Gatekeeper talent. Although for some reason it sent you off in a different direction, didn't it?'

Angela nodded. 'Tim... er... Timoth... wasn't there when we arrived but I knew how to find the village. We were heading there when Carradin and Jeznia found us.'

A *derralind*: that's what the Challendrians had called Angela. Tim wasn't surprised she'd been able to locate the village; *derralind* meant "finder" and Angela had led the Wardens to people or places on several occasions when she and Tim had last been in Challenrah.

'I need to work out how your companion came to be here with you,' Devron said to Angela, 'and why The Gate separated you and Timoth. Let's sit awhile and have some refreshment before we do anything else.'

The horse-thing had been standing patiently, tearing up mouthfuls of grass. It lifted its head now and nuzzled the Gatekeeper as he took some provisions from the bags on its back. Tim, Angela and Madison sat with Nashena on the grass near the fallen tree while Devron and the Wardens sorted out food and drinks from Devron's bags and their own backpacks. Jasper seemed to have calmed down at last. He lay down, tucked against Tim's legs. Nashena moved to sit near Madison and soon the two were deep in conversation.

'I almost didn't recognise Nashena,' Tim said to Angela.

'I know. She's nearly our age now. Carradin explained about the time change here. It feels strange, doesn't it?'

Tim leaned towards Angela and lowered his voice. 'He's different. Devron, I mean. He looks the same. He doesn't look any older. He's different, though.'

Angela smiled. 'He has his full powers back,' she said. 'He was ill when we were last here, wasn't he? I asked Carradin about him on the way here. Apparently, it took him months to recover from that poison.'

Saving Devron after he'd been wounded by a poisoned arrow had been Tim's first experience of using his special Gift for healing. 'I could have helped him get better more quickly if we'd stayed,' he said quietly.

'I'm sure you could have,' Angela agreed, 'but closing The Gate was more important to him. And to Challenrah.'

'Why?' Madison asked, breaking off from her chat with Nashena. 'What happened?'

'I'll tell you later,' Angela promised.

Tim glowered. It had been *their* adventure – his and Angela's. He wasn't sure he wanted Madison to know all about it, especially the part where he'd almost sided with the rebels.

Carradin passed some bread and cheese to Tim and he chewed without really tasting it. Why was Madison here with them? Devron had obviously sensed when Tim and the girls had entered Challenrah but even he didn't know why the new Gate had let her through, nor why they hadn't all been together when they'd arrived. He took another bite of food. What about that awful dream he'd had, the one with the boy – had it been Hamett? – shouting that everything was going wrong and Tim had to help? Tim gave Jasper a piece of cheese.

Before healing Jeznia, the Gatekeeper had telepathically said he'd speak with Tim in a moment. That was ages ago. Maybe Devron had worked it all out by now and would explain what was going on. Tim stood up and was on the point of going to talk to the Gatekeeper when he heard a noise like distant thunder, faint at first but growing louder by the second.

Chapter 5

A Ride to The Gate

An enormous dust cloud billowed towards the group at the edge of the village, bringing with it the ever-increasing, thunderous sound. Tim could barely hear Jasper's frightened whine above the thudding noise. He put his arms around the dog. Drawing close at great speed was a whole herd of the horse-things.

Devron left the group and stood in the path of the oncoming animals. He waited calmly as they slowed to a lumbering trot and then a gentle walk. They snorted and stamped their huge feet. The Gatekeeper walked amongst them as the dust settled. He patted each one and spoke to them. Tim couldn't hear what he said but the creatures must have understood, for three remained where they were while the rest spun round and raced away, raising dust again.

Devron returned to the group. 'I'd better go back to Vallend's Gate,' he said. 'Come with me, Carradin. You too, Jeznia. Let's see if between us we can convince The Gate to stay still long enough for us to send a Deemster through.'

'What's a Deemster?' Madison whispered to Angela.

'Someone who goes through a new Gate to explore what's on the other side,' Angela explained. 'If there are people there, a Deemster will try to find someone to be a Gatekeeper on that side of The Gate.'

'What if there aren't any people?' Madison asked.

Devron turned and answered. 'We explore, if it's safe, and let The Gate stay as long as it wants or, if necessary, shut it down. Enough questions for now. I have to go.'

What about us? Tim wondered. *Are we just supposed to wait here? We might as well go home if we're not needed.* At the last moment, he tried to hide his thoughts, blanketing them in a thick, fluffy cloud as Devron had taught him. He'd left it a bit too late.

Devron grinned. *I hadn't forgotten you.* 'You children will come with us,' he said aloud.

'We can't,' Tim said, although he desperately wanted to go with Devron. 'We have to be back before–'

'–before it's fully dark here,' Devron finished for him. 'I know.'

Tim blushed. Of course Devron knew that.

'I'll have you back in time,' the Gatekeeper said. 'Jeznia, take Anaga, will you? I'll take our newcomer. Timoth can ride with you, Carradin. Can you manage your little animal, Timoth? What is it?'

'A dog,' said Tim.

'Oh. I'd like to learn about it later. Take that one, Nashena,' he said, pointing to the smallest of the horse-things. He took rope bridles from the bags slung over his mount's back and handed them to Nashena.

'You can ride?' Tim asked her.

Nashena nodded. 'I've been riding since I was six.' She slipped a nose loop over each animal's muzzle and left the reins dangling.

The reason for the extra three mounts was clear now, but Tim wondered how the animals had known Devron needed them. He had no time to ask. Carradin helped Nashena onto the back of her animal, then assisted Jeznia onto another of the creatures before hoisting Angela up in front of her. He used the trunk of the fallen tree as a step to climb onto the third horse-thing and reached down a hand for Tim to pass Jasper up to him.

Tim hesitated. *Why does Madison get to ride with Devron? It's not fair. I need to ask him about The Gates and my dream.* He blanketed his thoughts hastily. He didn't want Devron to "hear" him complaining. He picked up a reluctant Jasper and passed him to Carradin, then he took hold of Carradin's hand and was swung up onto the red-grey back of the large mount. Surprisingly, Jasper settled quietly in Tim's arms. 'Good job you're no bigger!' Tim said to the dog. 'Carradin, what are these horse-things called?'

'Horse-things?' Carradin repeated. 'What's a horse?'

'It's… Never mind. What are we riding?'

'Temarals,' said Carradin.

'Oh. Right. And the cats?'

'Cats?'

It seemed strange to Tim that Carradin and Devron didn't know about cats and dogs but, then again, he hadn't asked about Larn's species, and hadn't known about temarals. 'Larn and Parrin and Syeesha,' he said. 'What are they?'

'Leodans,' Carradin said. 'Hush now and concentrate. Hold your animal – a dog, did you say? – with one arm and keep a firm grasp on the temaral's mane with the other.'

Devron lifted Madison onto the temaral he'd ridden to the village and then leapt up behind her. The animal snuffled and stamped. Devron quieted it with a hand on its neck. 'Everyone ready?' he asked, taking up the reins. 'Good. Let's go.'

Tim found the ride terrifying and exhilarating at the same time. The temaral walked with a sway that made him feel a bit sea-sick and its trot was really uncomfortable. Carradin apparently had no difficulty staying seated but only the Warden's strong arm around Tim's waist kept him safely on the animal's back when he lost his hold on the long, straggly mane as he clutched Jasper to stop him falling off.

Ahead of the group, Devron raised his hand in a signal and the real ride began. As one, the temarals lurched into a gallop, their huge feet pounding the dry ground as they sped along. Despite the speed and the temarals' ungainly feet, this galloping gait was unexpectedly smooth and Tim's sea-sickness faded away. He grasped the mane and Jasper more securely and started to enjoy himself.

Jasper wriggled. 'Keep still,' Tim shouted to him. 'What's wrong?'

The dog settled again and Tim saw what had disturbed him. Larn, Parrin and Syeesha were racing alongside the temarals, matching their pace with long, leaping strides. Larn's great ears flopped as he ran and his tongue lolled out of the side of his mouth. Tim laughed and the big cat – leodan, Tim reminded himself – looked up at him.

'Go, Larn!' Tim yelled. 'Good boy!' Behind him, Carradin chuckled and Tim squirmed in embarrassment. 'Sorry,' he muttered, taking a tighter hold of Jasper and the temaral's mane.

Tim didn't know exactly how long the ride lasted but the huge temarals were beginning to snort and pant as if they were tiring when Devron signalled again and the group slowed to a brief trot and then a sedate walk. This time Tim didn't feel sick – until they came in sight of The Gate.

It was in a meadow, with no dwellings visible in any direction. A low fence with no obvious purpose ran out from either side of The Gate for about a metre. As they drew nearer, Tim could see that this Gate was taller than both the old, faulty Gate and the new one he had come through today. It was made of six vertical wooden planks, with a cross-piece top and bottom, and a diagonal bar. The tops of the planks and gate posts were jagged points. From this distance, Tim couldn't tell whether or not there was a padlock on the latch. It looked to him as if The Gate was wobbling and blurring. All Tim could see through the gaps was a hazy darkness instead of the red-green grass of Challenrah. It was most peculiar and it made him quite queasy.

A bearded man and a woman were sitting on the grass a few metres away from The Gate. Both of them rose to their feet as Devron dismounted and walked towards them, leaving Madison standing by the temaral. The Gatekeeper spoke briefly to the man and then put his arms around the woman and kissed her forehead.

'Kallyn!' Nashena called, sliding down from her temaral and running to the woman. Kallyn pushed away from Devron and hugged her niece.

Carradin lowered Tim and Jasper to the ground before dismounting and going to help Angela and Jeznia. He took the bridles off all the mounts and the bags from Devron's temaral. The animals trotted away. 'They'll come back when Devron calls them,' he told Tim.

Tim grasped Jasper's leash and stared at The Gate. Larn and his parents dashed past him to lie, panting, near Devron. The Gatekeeper patted each of them. The leodans remained where they were as Devron gestured for the man (Vallend, Tim presumed) to accompany him closer to The Gate.

With Nashena at her side, Kallyn came to greet the Wardens before speaking to the children. 'It's good to see you, Timoth and Anaga,' she said. 'We've missed you.' She turned to Madison. 'A newcomer. Welcome.'

Tim pointed to The Gate. He wished it would stop quivering. 'That's not good, is it? Why won't it stay still?'

'It is still at the moment,' Kallyn said. 'It hasn't moved for a couple of days – except to try and open up.'

'No, it's not,' said Tim. 'It's sort of shaky and blurry. It's making me feel nauseous.'

'You're sure it's moving?'

'Yes. It's all wobbly.'

Kallyn looked from The Gate to Tim and back again. 'Devron! Vallend!' she shouted urgently. 'Get away from The Gate!'

Chapter 6

Attack

Devron and Vallend ran, the great cats at their heels. The Gate shook violently and shot a metre or so above the ground. Trailing its short fence like unwieldy tail-feathers, it took off after the two men. Vallend glanced over his shoulder and changed direction. The Gate ignored him and kept heading straight for Devron. The Gatekeeper glanced back then veered off, leading it away from the Wardens and the children.

Carradin grabbed Kallyn to prevent her from rushing to Devron's aid. 'Not yet,' he said.

Frightened though he was, Tim started forwards. It was an errant Gate. He should be able to help. Larn flattened him before he'd taken more than two steps. He struggled into a sitting position in time to see Devron turn and face The Gate.

The Gatekeeper raised both arms, with his palms out towards the oncoming threat. He shouted some words that Tim couldn't make out. The Gate slowed. Tim could see a faint, golden glow forming between The

Gate and the Gatekeeper. The Gate shuddered to a halt in mid-air, with the flimsy fence touching the ground.

'Get over here, Vallend!' Devron yelled, and the other Gatekeeper ran to his side.

Carradin released Kallyn, and they and Jeznia raced across the grass to stand with the Gatekeepers. The golden glow intensified.

Tim tried to stand up to go and join them but Larn sank his huge fangs into the leg of his jeans and held on firmly. Syeesha and Parrin positioned themselves near the three terrified girls.

It ended as quickly as it had started. One moment The Gate was looming over the Gatekeepers and Wardens, the next it was back on the ground, with the short fence settled neatly to either side. Larn let go of Tim's jeans.

Tim stood up and brushed at the slobber on his leg. 'Yuck, Larn,' he said. 'Thought you'd have stopped slobbering now you've grown up.' The leodan stalked away. 'Jasper!' Tim called out, suddenly panicking. 'Jasper!'

The dog bounded forward from wherever he'd been hiding and leapt at Tim in a frenzy of greeting. Larn turned and padded back to Tim. Jasper quivered but stood his ground as Larn approached. The two animals touched noses and Jasper wagged his tail. Larn snuffled at the dog's ears before strolling off again. Tim let out a breath he hadn't realised he'd been holding.

'I think you can let him off that restraint now,' Nashena said, coming over to Tim. 'We let animals run free here and the leodans won't harm him now he and Larn are friends.' Tim hesitated. 'He won't get lost,'

Nashena assured him as Angela and Madison joined them. 'Larn will look after him.'

Tim unclipped the leash from Jasper's collar. 'Good job Devron *does* have his full powers, isn't it?' he said to Angela.

'It *was* a bit scary,' Angela admitted.

Madison grimaced. 'That's an understatement.'

Despite his resentment at her being here at all, Tim was grudgingly impressed by Madison's attitude. He knew from his own experience just how strange and confusing it was to find yourself in a different world. Madison hadn't complained – at least, not in his hearing – and she hadn't pestered with hundreds of questions. Angela had probably explained a bit about Challenrah, but Madison must be both curious and scared. He was about to show off some of his knowledge about Gates when he noticed the pendant around her neck.

'Where did you get that?'

'Get what?' Madison asked.

'The pendant?'

'Oh. Carradin gave it to me as soon as we met him and Jeznia. Why? What's special about it?'

'They didn't tell you?'

Madison shook her head. 'There wasn't much time to talk. He just said I was to wear it.'

Tim decided that for once he'd answer her properly. 'It makes you look like a Challendrian,' he said, pointing out his own pendant and the one around Angela's neck. 'To everyone except Wardens and Gatekeepers, of course.'

'Oh,' Madison said again. 'Okay.'

Tim stared at her. She didn't seem at all fazed by the idea of a magical pendant.

'After that man – Devron – healing that woman's arm,' she said, 'and then the flying gate, I'll believe anything of this place.'

Tim was about to point out that he'd helped Jeznia first, when Devron, Kallyn and the Wardens came back from The Gate, leaving Vallend by it.

'It's safe for the time being,' Devron said, leading the group farther away. 'Well done for noticing the danger, Timoth.'

'I didn't...' Tim began, but saw Madison watching him and changed what he was going to say. 'It was sort of shivering and it looked blurred,' he said. That part was true. 'I knew something bad was going to happen.' That part wasn't.

Devron gave Tim a considered look but made no comment. Tim turned away hastily and patted Jasper.

'Never seen a Gate do that before,' Carradin said.

Devron nodded agreement. 'Neither have I.'

'So how did you know what to do?' Jeznia asked.

'Just took a chance,' Devron said. 'It was a bit close for comfort, though, until you all joined in. I'd stopped it, but I doubt I'd have managed to settle it back down without help.'

Madison leaned close to Angela and whispered a question. 'That other man's supposed to be in charge of that gate, isn't he? Why didn't *he* stop it?'

Nashena answered before Angela could reply. 'Devron's stronger,' she said proudly. 'He's the best Gatekeeper on Challenrah. He's my uncle. Kallyn's my aunt. She's strong, too. She's a Senior Warden – like Carradin and Jeznia. Devron's the best Gatekeeper ever.'

'Not so, little one,' said Devron, ruffling his niece's dark hair. 'Your mother was better.'

'About that Gate…' said Carradin.

'I don't see how I can leave it,' Devron said. 'I'll have to send Vallend to tend Timoth's Gate and stay with this one.'

'Why do they speak of the gate as if "the gate" is a name, like "The Gate" with a capital T and G?' Madison asked quietly.

'Because Gates are special,' Tim whispered back. 'Shut up, Madison.'

'How am I going to learn about this place if I don't ask things?'

That was just how Tim had felt when he'd first arrived in Challenrah and, if he was honest, for much of the time during his visits. Right now, he was more interested in listening to Devron and the Wardens than talking to Madison. 'Just keep quiet,' he hissed, and turned his attention back to the Gatekeeper.

Devron glanced up at the sky. The orange sun was past its mid-point but still high overhead. 'You and the girls can stay a while longer,' he said to Tim. 'I'll make sure you're back before dark. Vallend can go with you.'

Tim wanted Devron to be the one looking after the new Gate, not Vallend, but he didn't dare complain. What if he pretended there was some problem with his new Gate? Maybe that would change Devron's mind.

'There's no problem with your Gate, is there, Timoth?' Devron asked.

'No,' Tim said promptly. 'Not that I know of.' He really must remember to cloud his thoughts when Devron was around. 'Sorry.'

'You do realise how important it is that I sort out this Gate?'

Tim nodded. 'Can I help?'

'I'm not sure,' said Devron.

A wave of relief washed through Tim. At least the Gatekeeper hadn't dismissed the idea or sent him away because The Gate might become dangerous again. 'Can I ask you something?' he ventured.

'Ask away,' said Devron.

'How many Gates are there?'

'Seven, at the moment,' the Gatekeeper said.

'Seven? Isn't that a lot? I thought only three or four ever formed at one time?'

'It's unusual,' Devron said, 'but most of them don't lead anywhere. They're harmless and not causing any trouble. A Gatekeeper is guarding each of them, except for yours. Wardens are looking after that one for now. Three Gates are fading at present but I can feel another trying to form. Sometimes they don't manage it. Gateways often weaken and die away before they can become established.'

'You can sense all these Gates, even if they're far away?'

'Yes. But Gateways only form across one area of Challenrah – a very large area, granted, but not across our whole world. They're usually within about a three-day ride from my village, so under normal circumstances it's possible for me to get there if another Gatekeeper needs help.'

'And this Gate is the only problem one at the moment?'

'Fortunately, yes.' He frowned. 'This one's hard enough to deal with. I don't want extra complications.'

'Devron,' Kallyn called. 'Come. It's way past midday and high time we all had a rest and some refreshment. You can discuss all this while we're eating.'

'Where does this Gate lead?' Tim asked as he walked with Devron to where Kallyn and the Wardens were setting out food and drinks taken from their packs. Tim grabbed Jasper's collar and hauled him back as he tried to stuff his nose into one of the packs.

'We're not sure,' Devron said. 'When it first formed and opened, Vallend caught a glimpse of a land beyond but everything was hazy. Since then, it's been too unstable to let it open again.'

'But it's trying to open now?' Tim persisted. 'I heard you say Vallend was having difficulty keeping it shut.' He frowned as an unpleasant, pushing sensation started to build up in his head. 'Can you feel that?' he asked Devron.

'Feel what?'

'A sort of pressure. It hurts my head.'

'Pressure?' Devron repeated. He swung round and looked at The Gate. 'Good lad! Well noticed. Everyone stay here!' He sprinted towards The Gate. 'Vallend! Look out!'

Tim watched in horror as it burst open, with a blast of air that sent both Vallend and Devron flying backwards to land heavily on the red-tinted grass.

Chapter 7

An Unruly Gate

Kallyn was the first to reach Devron. The others rushed up as he clambered to his feet and brushed dirt from his face.

'I'm all right,' he told his wife. 'Timoth, can you help Vallend? I need to close that Gate.'

Tim stared at the open Gate. Whatever was beyond it was shrouded in a swirling mist but there were definitely creatures of some kind there. He could see small, shadowy shapes flitting around, battering like moths around a light-bulb at the hazy barrier between Challenrah and wherever the other place was. He didn't like the feel of it, and he certainly didn't like the look of the grey, gauzy tendrils of mist that were slowly weaving their way through The Gate towards Devron.

'Timoth!' Devron said sharply.

Tim hurried to obey. He knelt by the fallen Gatekeeper and ran a hand gently from the man's head to his waist. He couldn't detect any serious injury, just bruising and shock. He rested his hand on Vallend's chest and let his healing talent flow slowly into the man's body.

Vallend took a deep breath. 'That's much better,' he said. 'Move aside, lad. I need to help Devron.' He stood up and joined Devron and the Wardens.

He might have said thank you, Tim thought sourly, hastily blanketing the complaint. He stalked away to stand with Angela, Madison and Nashena.

'I may not have Gatekeeper talent like you,' Angela said, 'but even I can tell that's not good, is it?' She pointed to the open Gate and the coils of mist.

Tim shook his head. The uncomfortable pressure had eased but he could still feel a kind of throbbing coming from The Gate. Desperate to go and help, but wary of interfering, he stayed where he was. A quick glance around told him that Jasper was with Larn, a safe distance away.

Something zoomed past his face and he jerked back with a yelp of alarm. Had some of that mist already reached this far? A buzz sounded by his right ear and something brushed against his neck. He swatted it away and darted round to see what it was. He caught a glimpse of a dark-purple body, translucent wings and long, floaty legs.

'What *are* you doing?' Angela asked.

'It was one of those fly-things,' he said. 'Like the one I saw when we were in the dog park. You must have seen it this time.'

'No,' said Angela 'Oh, look. Devron's shut The Gate.'

'What? How?'

'I don't know how. You distracted me. You should have been watching.'

'I was. Until that fly-thing buzzed past me. They're huge. How can you *not* see them?'

'He just walked up and closed it,' Madison said.

'That's a very helpful explanation.'

Tim's sarcasm didn't seem to bother Madison. She shrugged and said, 'Well, that's what he did.'

Irritated, Tim turned his back on her and walked a few paces towards The Gate. He stood staring at it. The wobbliness and blurring had gone and the tendrils of mist had disappeared. It looked like any other wooden gate – except that it was stuck out here in the middle of nowhere.

Devron stood for several minutes with his hand on The Gate before calling the Wardens and Vallend away. 'It's safe for now,' he said as he and the other adults joined the children, 'and I for one could do with something to eat. Vallend, let me know if you see or sense anything amiss. You too, Timoth.'

Tim's irritation at Madison and Vallend vanished. Devron trusted him to help keep a check on The Gate and that was more than enough to satisfy him for the moment.

Angela tapped him on the shoulder. 'What are we going to call her?'

'Call who?'

'Madison. She needs a Challendrian name while she's here, doesn't she?'

'I suppose so,' Tim agreed. 'Let's ask Nashena.'

'I heard,' Nashena said. 'How about Madria?'

'Madria. I like that,' Madison said. 'I wonder if Devron's worked out why we didn't come through The Gate with you, Tim?'

'It's Timoth when we're here,' Tim said, 'and in case you hadn't noticed, he's been rather busy.'

He did want to know the reason his Gate had separated them, though, and why it had let Madison through in the first place. And why was it, he mused as they all settled to eat, that he was always so annoyed with Madison? When he and his mother and Peter, and his baby sister Cassie, had moved to California and he'd started school in Oceanside, he was in the same class as Madison but they hadn't taken much notice of each other. Only when Angela joined the class half-way through the year had Madison made a special effort to become friends with them both.

'I thought you weren't coming, after all,' he said to Angela.

She looked blankly at him. 'What?'

'To the States. To Oceanside. I thought you'd already be here when we arrived but it was months later.'

'I texted you and FaceTimed often enough,' Angela reminded him. 'You knew it was taking Granddad longer than we'd expected to be fit enough to travel.'

'It just seemed a long wait, that's all. There was no one else I could talk to about Challenrah.'

'What happened last time you were here?' Madison asked.

Devron's arrival saved Tim from replying. Food in hand, the Gatekeeper sat on the grass next to Nashena. Angela, Tim and Madison shuffled closer.

'I don't yet know why you're here, Madria,' he said. 'Yes, I heard Nashena's name for you. It means "maker". I suspect you have some talent that's not shown itself yet – some Gift that we're going to need.'

'You can tell if someone has a special talent?' Madison asked.

'Only once it has begun to develop,' Devron replied. 'Most Gifts start to show when a person is between ten and fourteen years old. There are exceptions, though. Anyway, young Madria, I'm sure we'll find out about you soon enough. I do, however, know why you and Anaga came through to a different location.'

Tim leaned forward eagerly. Had the new Gate wanted him to go to the village to meet Nashena first? Anaga was a "finder"; had The Gate wanted her to find something or someone on a different route to the village?

Devron smiled. 'Nothing complicated, as it turns out. Timoth's Gate is very new and it's just settling in. I was occupied with Vallend's Gate, there was no other Gatekeeper available, and Evrald's team hadn't reached it when Timoth opened it. Timoth has Gatekeeper talents developing so it let him through. Because you were with him and Anaga, it tried to let you all through at the same time but couldn't quite manage it.'

'So we ended up somewhere different?' Angela said.

'Exactly.'

Madison chuckled. 'A baby Gate.'

Devron laughed. 'That's a good way to describe it. Some Gates are efficient straight away; others take longer to work properly.'

'And some don't work well at all,' Tim commented, looking over to Vallend's Gate.

'How true,' Devron agreed.

He started eating and Tim and the others sat quietly for a while, concentrating on their own food. Tim took a bite of something that looked like dark-brown bread but tasted more like very spicy cake. He grimaced and held it out for Jasper. The dog sniffed it suspiciously and then wolfed it down before sidling across to Devron and lying with his head on the Gatekeeper's leg. Devron stroked Jasper's soft fur. Tim ate some cheese instead, along with a slice of what he knew was Kallyn's home-baked, tasty bread.

'A dog, did you say?' Devron asked, and Tim nodded, his mouth too full of food to answer properly.

Devron tickled Jasper's ears, then pushed him gently aside and stood up. 'It's time you went back,' he said. 'I'll call the temarals.' He stood for a moment as if deep in thought. 'Right,' he said. 'They'll be here shortly.'

'How...?' Madison began, but Devron had called Vallend over and wasn't listening to her.

'I'll stay here with Kallyn and Carradin,' he said to Vallend. 'I'd like you to take the children back to the new Gate. Jeznia can go with you. Nashena, too. Her brother's in Evrald's team. She'll be safe with them.'

So that's where Hamett is. Tim made sure he was clouding his thoughts. He wasn't trying to keep anything from Devron this time but he'd decided to practise concealing his thoughts in case he needed to do so in the future.

'I'd prefer to remain here,' Vallend said. 'I know this Gate's quirks by now.'

'I'm sure you do,' Devron agreed, 'but it's thrown us a few surprises today, hasn't it?'

Vallend frowned. 'I can cope. My team will be back soon.'

'And I'll send them on to you,' Devron said. 'Evrald's team can then join me here.'

'I've been your Second for nearly a year,' Vallend said. 'You know I'm capable.'

Devron's expression hardened. 'What I *do* know is that you should have called me in as soon as that Gate started trying to force its way open and you couldn't keep it closed.' He held up a hand. 'Let's not argue over this. The new Gate needs tending. It was fine for a while but it's become unsettled now Timoth isn't nearby and it won't be happy when he's back in his world. You know how tricky they can be when they're not stabilised.'

Vallend looked as if he was going to object again but after a moment's hesitation he nodded. 'If that's what you want.'

'It's the best solution for the time being,' Devron said. 'The nearest Gatekeeper I could call in for Timoth's Gate is Grentha and she's not strong enough to stabilise it. Once you've steadied it, you can bring her in to guard it and you can get back here to help me.'

Everyone turned at the sound of the temarals approaching. Tim saw that there were just three this time: the ones Nashena and Jeznia had ridden and a sturdy, silvery-coated one that he'd not seen before.

'Anaga,' Devron said, 'you have good balance. Have you ridden before?'

'I used to go horse-riding quite often,' she replied.

'I presume a horse is a mount back in your world?'

Angela nodded. 'It's a bit different riding a temaral, though. Even our large horses are smaller than the temarals.'

'Ride with Nashena,' Devron instructed. 'You'll be fine. Jeznia, take Madria, will you? Timoth can ride with Vallend.' He grinned at the other Gatekeeper. 'This young man will doubtless have plenty of questions for you about Gates.'

Reluctant though he was to leave, Tim was beginning to worry about the time. It would be a long ride back and he needed to be home before he was missed. Vallend mounted the silver temaral and Devron lifted Tim up in front while Carradin helped the others who were to return to the new Gate. Tim reached down for Jasper. Devron picked up the dog and held him close, stroking him for a moment or two before handing him to Tim. Devron's touch seemed to calm Jasper for he settled in Tim's grasp almost immediately.

With a few words of farewell, Vallend and his group set off. From his hiding place in the long grass, Larn appeared and bounded after the temarals. He drew level with Vallend's mount and kept pace alongside as they journeyed on.

Tim had hoped to talk with Vallend about The Gates but, even though he found the ride easier this time, he had to concentrate hard to keep his balance while holding Jasper. He did venture one or two questions but Vallend wasn't very communicative.

'Wait till we reach The Gate,' the Gatekeeper said. 'I'll talk with you then.'

Tim relaxed and tried to enjoy the rest of the ride.

They had just come in sight of Devron's village when Madison shouted for help.

Chapter 8

Late Home

'Hold tight!' Vallend shouted.

Tim grabbed the temaral's mane and gripped Jasper firmly as the Gatekeeper swung his mount round and urged it close to Jeznia and Madison. Leaving Tim on the animal's back, he leapt down in time to catch Jeznia as she slumped sideways and slid off her temaral. Tim leaned over to lower Jasper to the ground and then jumped down.

He bent and rubbed his ankle. 'Ouch. Long drop.' He glared up at the huge temaral. The animal snorted and stamped a few paces away.

The pain in his ankle faded quickly and he hurried over to where Vallend was kneeling by Jeznia. Nashena and Angela dismounted and came to stand nearby.

'Hey!' Madison called. 'Don't leave me up here!'

Nashena ran over to help her down from the temaral.

Tim could see that Jeznia was deathly pale. Her breathing was shallow and laboured.

Vallend had his hand on her forehead. 'Anyone know what's caused this?'

'She was stung by something,' Tim said. 'On her left arm. I helped her a bit, then Devron healed her but he said there was still infection there. She was supposed to tell us if she felt unwell again.'

Vallend rolled up Jeznia's sleeve to reveal an arm that was red and swollen. The nasty blisters hadn't returned but the inflammation looked awful. Tim's instinct was to rush in and help but he was unsure how Vallend would react. All Gatekeepers were healers; he knew that, but he didn't know how good Vallend was. The Gatekeeper was Devron's Second – his deputy – so surely he must have strong powers. He'd have more experience than Tim, too, wouldn't he?

Vallend closed his eyes in concentration. Tim stood by, fidgeting slightly. It seemed ages before Jeznia's breathing eased and colour returned to her face.

The Gatekeeper opened his eyes and sat back on his heels. 'Come over here, Timoth.'

Tim knelt down by him. Jeznia's arm was still red but there was less swelling.

Vallend used his sleeve to wipe sweat from his face. 'This should have healed properly. There's something wrong.'

'That's what Devron said when he couldn't clear all the infection,' Tim said. 'What d'you want me to do?'

Vallend glanced at him. 'You're already quite a strong healer.' Tim raised his eyebrows in surprise. Had Devron told Vallend about him or could Vallend also sense talent? 'See if you can reduce the swelling any more,' the Gatekeeper continued. 'I'll take over again in a few minutes if necessary.'

He pushed himself up and went to fetch a flask from one of the packs. Tim turned his attention to the Warden.

It hadn't been easy to heal Devron and Hamett in the past, but that was partly because Tim hadn't really known what he was doing. It had been trial and error. Devron's instructions had helped but Tim was still new at this. Nevertheless, he concentrated hard and was thankful to see a gradual improvement in Jeznia. The swelling disappeared but the red mark at the site of the sting refused to fade. Tim knew he couldn't heal her any further. He took his hand off her arm. As Devron and Vallend had observed, there was something wrong and unusual about that sting.

Vallend helped Jeznia to sit up and held the flask for her while she drank. 'You should have told me about your arm,' he scolded gently. 'I could have stopped it getting that bad.'

Jeznia gave a weak smile. 'It came on very quickly this time. It started prickling but I thought I'd be all right until we reached The Gate. The next thing I remember is being on the ground with you kneeling by me.'

'Let's get you home,' Vallend said, supporting her as she stood up. 'Nashena, can you "communicate" yet?'

'Only with Devron and Hamett,' Nashena replied, 'and a bit with Kallyn, but I can "talk" to them over quite a distance now.'

'Good. I'll leave you with Jeznia at her home while I take these children to The Gate. You can ask Hamett to tell me if I'm needed urgently.'

'It's getting dark,' Tim said anxiously.

Vallend shrugged. 'So I see, and I'm afraid it'll be darker by the time we reach The Gate. The temarals won't come into the village so we'll have to walk from here. They'll meet us again at the other side.'

'Will they know the way? To The Gate, I mean? I don't know how to get to this new Gate. I can't remember the way I came to the village.' Tim realised he was babbling but he couldn't help it; the sun was sinking fast and he had to get home.

'I thought you had more knowledge of Gates and Gatekeepers,' Vallend said, and Tim felt the blood rush to his face. Vallend shrugged dismissively. 'I can find any Gate on Challenrah,' he declared.

'So can I,' Angela added softly.

'Sorry,' Tim said. 'It's just that I have to go home because–'

'Time will move on for you in your world,' Vallend interrupted. 'I know. There's nothing I can do about that. You'll just have to deal with the consequences when you're back there.' He slipped his arm around Jeznia and led her off into the village.

Nashena took the packs and reins off the temarals. 'Here,' she said, handing a pack each to Madison, Angela and Tim.

The temarals ambled away, with Larn following them.

'Where's Larn going?' Madison asked.

'The leodans won't come into the village without Devron,' Angela told her. 'I expect Larn will join us again later. He seems to like being with Timoth.'

'Can't imagine why,' Madison muttered.

Tim turned his back on her. He hoisted the pack over his shoulder and started off after Vallend and Jeznia. 'Why can't we go on to The Gate without them?' he asked Angela. 'You can find it.'

'Will it let us back out?' Angela asked.

'Oh. Good point,' Tim said. 'I'm not sure. It wouldn't open when I tried just after I'd got here.'

'So, we need Vallend, don't we?'

'S'pose so,' Tim agreed. He looked down at his dog. 'Come on, then, Jasper. We'll just have to hope no one misses us, won't we?'

'Worrying about getting back won't make us get there any faster,' Madison observed, quickening her stride to keep up with Tim, Angela and Nashena.

'Very helpful,' Tim retorted. Angela jabbed him in the ribs with her elbow. 'Ow! What was that for?'

'What's the matter with you?' Angela demanded. 'I thought you'd be happy to be back here but all you've done is grumble at Madria. And don't say it's because you're worried about getting home before it's fully dark here. You've been like this since we arrived.'

'It's all right for you,' Tim said, ignoring her comment about his attitude toward Madison. 'Your mother knows all about Challenrah. So does David. It doesn't matter if you don't get home in time.'

'Who's David?' Madison asked.

'My grandfather,' Angela replied. 'He was the Gatekeeper on our side of the old Gate back in England, until he was ill and Timoth had to help instead.'

'What about your dad?' asked Madison. 'Does he know about this place as well?'

Angela nodded. 'He's never been here but we've told him all about it.'

Trailing along after the Gatekeeper and Warden, Tim wondered what his mother and Peter would say if he told them about Challenrah. They wouldn't believe him; he was sure of that. They'd think it was his imagination again: another of the stories he liked to write.

Jeznia seemed to improve further as they walked through the quiet village. She and Vallend greeted the few people they encountered but no one stopped to chat. Tim was grateful for that; he was growing increasingly anxious about the time.

'At last,' he muttered as they came to Jeznia's cottage, just a few doors down from Devron's.

'I'll be fine,' Jeznia assured Vallend. 'Go. Get the children back home.'

Vallend checked her arm once more. 'If there's the slightest change, tell Nashena to "inform" Hamett. He can tell me and I'll come right back.'

Tim sidled closer to Angela. 'Can all the Gatekeepers and Wardens communicate by telepathy?'

Angela nodded. 'Hamett once told me that some are better at it than others.'

Tim grimaced. 'So any of them can tell what we're thinking?'

'No. It doesn't work like that. Hamett said you usually have to have their consent before you can communicate with anyone through telepathy. Then you have to deliberately "send" your thoughts to someone for them to "hear" you. They can't pick up random thoughts from just anyone. Well, most of them can't.'

'Devron can, if he chooses to,' Tim said.

Angela smiled. 'That doesn't surprise me. He's the Leader, isn't he?'

'The Leader?' Madison repeated.

'The chief Gatekeeper. He's in charge. Come on; Vallend's calling us.'

Tim trotted after her. He'd once been told by an amused Devron that he was "thinking loudly". It would appear that someone strong in telepathy could pick up those thoughts. He was glad he'd been practising his concealing cloud. He didn't want Vallend, or anyone else, to know what he was thinking unless he gave them his permission.

As Vallend had promised, the temarals were waiting for them when they left the village, although there were only two of them. Larn was there too. He bounded forward and Tim dodged behind a temaral to avoid being knocked down again.

'Stop it, Larn,' he said. The feline growled a soft protest before turning to sniff gently at Jasper.

'How are we going to manage with just two mounts?' Madison asked.

Tim wanted to know that, too, but he was sick of being glared at when he kept asking questions. Let Madison chance it this time.

'You'll ride with me,' Vallend said to her. 'Anaga and Timoth, ride together. You're both competent enough for a short journey. That animal of yours – what did you say it was?'

'A dog,' Tim supplied.

'Right. Your dog can run by you. It's not far and Larn will look after it.'

With the sky darkening rapidly, it was difficult to make out any landmarks during the brief ride to The Gate. Tim doubted he'd be able to find his way to and from this new Gate without help.

'Why have we stopped?' he asked when the temarals halted.

'The temarals won't go any nearer to The Gate,' Vallend replied, lifting Madison down. He walked over and helped Tim and Angela to dismount.

'They went closer to that other Gate,' Tim pointed out.

'Devron was there,' Vallend said curtly. He took the reins from the temarals and patted the animals on their sturdy shoulders. 'Go,' he said, and the temarals raced away.

'How far...?' Tim began, but the Gatekeeper was striding onwards.

Stumbling in the darkness on the uneven ground, Tim hurried to keep up. It wasn't long before a faint, yellowy-gold glow lit the darkness ahead.

'It's The Gate,' he whispered in awe.

Vallend turned back to him. 'You've not seen a working, controlled Gate, have you? Evrald and his team have done a good job. It's almost stabilised already. They glow like this from time to time – on Challenrah anyway. I don't know if they do that on your world.'

'I've seen one glow and change colour,' Tim said, forgetting for the moment his haste to return home, 'but I don't think everyone can see that happen. The Gate, Vallend... It looks–' he searched for the right word '– happy.'

Vallend laughed. It was the first time the Gatekeeper had seemed amused by anything and Tim thought it made him seem more approachable.

'Well, it does!' he said defensively.

'I wouldn't have described it quite like that,' Vallend said, 'but it's a good way to put it. There's Evrald. Come, let's get you home.'

Hamett was supposed to be here somewhere, wasn't he? Tim wanted to see and speak with him but the sun had set and there was no time for anything more than a hurried greeting from Evrald. Sudden raindrops spattered around them as Vallend placed his hand on The Gate.

'There's no one too close on your side,' he said. 'Go through now, and remember to lock it behind you.'

Like Devron, Vallend needed no key. He simply placed one hand on the padlock and then unlatched The Gate. He pushed it open just wide enough for Tim and the others to slip through. Jasper dashed past Tim as The Gate closed.

Standing just a few metres away from The Gate was Tim's step-dad.

Chapter 9

Grounded

Peter was facing away from The Gate and no one else was nearby. Fumbling in his haste, Tim managed to slip the padlock through the ends of the chain. It snapped shut with a loud click.

Peter turned round. 'Where on earth have you been, Timothy?' He sounded both cross and worried. 'I've been out looking for you for the past hour.'

Tim glanced down at his watch. As usual, it had started working again as soon as he was back. He was about to protest that he hadn't been gone long but his watch told a different tale. He'd left home at six-thirty; it was now almost ten o'clock.

'I'm really sorry...' he began, but his step-dad was clearly in no mood to listen to any excuses.

'What's wrong with your phone?' Peter demanded. 'Did you forget to charge it? Your mum and I have been calling you. And why are you wet?'

Tim reached up and brushed at his head. His hair and the shoulders of his tee-shirt were damp. It wasn't raining on the Strand. 'I…' he started.

'Never mind,' Peter snapped. 'Come on. The car's over there. You too, girls. I'll drop you home Angela, but… Madison, is it? – you'll have to tell me where your house is. I'm surprised at the three of you, staying out this late. It's dark out here!' He paused to text Tim's mother, then said sharply, 'And get that dog on a lead. They're not allowed to run free here. I thought you knew that!'

'It's "leash",' Tim muttered under his breath.

Peter glanced at him. 'What did you say?'

'Nothing,' Tim answered. 'Just talking to Jasper.' He clipped the leash onto the dog's collar and followed his step-dad to the car. Peter ushered the children and Jasper into the back.

'What are you going to tell your parents?' Tim whispered to Madison as Peter started the car.

'Nothing,' said Madison. 'My dad died last year. It's just Mom and she's at work.'

'She leaves you alone at home?' Tim knew he didn't always appreciate having his mother and Peter checking on him so often but mostly he was glad they were around.

'No,' Madison said. 'Caleb's there. My brother. He's sixteen.'

'Won't he have missed you?'

Madison shook her head. 'He'll be on his computer. He'll just tell me I'm late and to get to bed before Mom comes home.'

Tim didn't need to ask Angela what she'd say. Her dad was away again on business but she'd be able to tell her mother and grandfather all about Challenrah. He wasn't sure how to feel about that. On the one hand, it would be good not to have to keep secrets; on the other, he rather enjoyed having something so special all to himself.

He didn't enjoy the consequences of being late back through The Gate, though.

'A whole week?' he protested when his mother grounded him.

'You've no idea how worried we were,' Lil said. 'And saying your watch stopped is no excuse.'

'It's true,' Tim said.

'You know very well you have to keep your phone charged.' It *had* been charged but, like his watch, it stopped working in Challenrah. He could hardly tell that to his mother. He tried not to look sulky as she went on, 'Apart from school and walking Jasper, you're stuck here for the week.'

'But...'

'But nothing. You're lucky it's not for longer, and that's only because it's the first time you've done something like this since we moved here.'

'But, Mum...' he tried again.

'What time are you supposed to be in at the weekend?'

Tim looked down at the floor. She was talking to him as if he was six, not almost twelve. 'Eight-thirty,' he mumbled.

'And Angela or that other girl–'

'Madison,' said Tim.

'Madison. One of them must have had a mobile phone.'

'They call them cell phones,' Tim corrected, unwisely. Lil glared at him. 'Sorry,' Tim muttered.

'Bed,' ordered his mother. 'We'll discuss this tomorrow.'

Tim had been out with Angela and Madison for just over three hours on this side of The Gate but had spent a whole day in Challenrah. He was exhausted. Jasper curled up in his basket at the side of Tim's bed and was snoring softly within minutes. Tired though he was, Tim took longer to drift off to sleep. Each time he was on the point of dropping off, he jerked awake thinking he heard Devron calling him.

He slept at last, only to find himself in a nightmare. He was in Challenrah again, standing not far from Vallend's Gate and it was raining hard. Somehow, Tim knew he was asleep but he couldn't force himself to wake from the dream. As he watched, The Gate opened slowly to reveal that peculiar, misty barrier beyond which flitted the strange, darting shapes. The mist thinned and the shapes took form. They were huge, winged, insect-type creatures like the ones Tim had seen in the dog park and in Challenrah. There were hundreds of them: too many to count and moving too fast. Through The Gate and into Challenrah they came in a gigantic swarm, twisting and turning before zooming off towards Tim's new Gate. As they passed, the grass and wild flowers below them withered and died.

Horrified, Tim could only stand and watch as the swarm disappeared briefly before returning moments later to circle around him where he stood near Vallend's Gate. Devron was by The Gate, although he'd not been there just seconds ago, and Tim stared in dismay as the Gatekeeper tried in vain to send the creatures back to their own land. The swarm attacked, smothering the Gatekeeper until all Tim could see was a writhing mass of darkness. Screaming for the creatures to leave Devron alone, Tim struggled to run forwards. He took two steps, tripped, and woke.

Jasper was standing with his head resting on the bed. Tim guessed he'd shouted in his sleep and disturbed the young dog.

'That was worse than the last dream,' he told Jasper. The dog wagged his tail and jumped onto the bed. Tim let him settle there. It was comforting to feel the warm, furry body close to him. Even with Jasper's soothing presence, it was quite a while before Tim fell asleep again.

'Grounded, eh?' said Madison. 'Tough luck.'

'Only for a week,' Tim said, trying to sound as if he didn't care. 'It's Monday already, isn't it? So just five more days to go.'

'At least you've got us for company,' Angela said brightly. 'Your Mum was happy enough for us to come back to your house after school today, wasn't she?'

'Yeah, because we're working on the bee-project. Hang on. I'll just take Cassie out to Mum.'

Madison tickled the little girl, making her giggle. 'Let her stay.'

Tim shook his head. 'She'll want the crayons and probably try to eat them.' He picked her up and carried the protesting toddler out of the room.

He returned moments later and his ill-humour evaporated as he and the girls settled round the table to begin planning how to set out their work.

Our class visit to the Buena Vista Audubon Society and Nature Centre started it all, he wrote. He crossed out *centre* and wrote *center*. 'Can't get used to your spellings,' he told Madison. 'Why d'you change the "e" and "r" round in "centre" and "metre"? Why d'you leave the "u" out of "flavour" and "colour"?'

'Stop it, Tim,' Angela said. 'We need to get on with this. We could win, you know. With our research and Madison's illustrations, I bet we stand a good chance.'

Tim studied the notes he'd made during the recent school trip. 'Seventy out of the top hundred human food crops are pollinated by bees. Wow! No wonder people are worried about losing the bees.'

'"In the US – among crops that require bee pollination – the number of bee colonies per hectare has declined by 90 percent since 1962",' Angela read out from her notebook.

Madison looked up from the honey bee picture she'd started. 'What's a hectare?'

'I looked that up,' Tim said. 'It's about the size of two football fields.'

'American football or soccer?'

'Soccer,' Tim answered. 'That's about forty tennis courts, or as big as a Major League Baseball field.'

Madison grinned. 'Oh. Okay.' She went back to her drawing.

'If we start with all the facts about the problem,' Tim said, 'with the statistics and the reasons we're losing the bees…'

'Then we can write about ways people like us can help,' Angela said.

'Make a bee garden,' Madison suggested without looking up.

Angela and Tim spoke together. 'A what?'

'I was taking notes as well,' Madison said smugly. 'Some bare ground for native bees, twig piles for bee nests, a bee house and plants that flower at different times of the year.'

The three of them worked on until Madison checked her watch and announced, 'Got to go. Caleb's picking me up.' She gathered her notes, sketch pad and pencils and stuffed them into her backpack. 'See you at school tomorrow.' She slung her pack over her shoulder and left the house.

Tim put down his pen. 'I have to take Jasper out, Angela. Want to come?'

Angela nodded. Tim went to tell his mother that he was going out with the dog, then he and Jasper and Angela headed for the Strand.

'Are we going as far as the pier?' Angela asked.

Tim shook his head. 'Haven't got time. And dogs aren't allowed on there.'

'Did you know it's the longest wooden pier on the California coast?' Angela said. 'It's a third of a mile long.'

'I did know, yes. Peter looked up all sorts of facts when we knew we were moving to Oceanside.'

'We have to get back to Challenrah,' Angela said suddenly.

'I know that too, but I'm grounded,' Tim retorted. 'School, dog-walking and home. That's it for the rest of the week.'

'But the dream you told me about – with Devron and those flying things?'

'It was just that,' Tim said. 'A dream. A nasty one, but just a dream. We thought there was something wrong after my last dream about Challenrah, didn't we? And there wasn't.'

'Apart from a terrifying Gate,' Angela said.

'Yeah, well, there was that. And the crops failing.'

'But the grass looked fine. You said it was dying, and Hamett called you – in that first dream.'

'I know. We didn't get to see Hamett, did we?'

'I think he was somewhere around, not far from the new Gate,' Angela said. 'I could have found him but there wasn't time.'

'*You* could go,' Tim said. He didn't want to be left behind but he'd disobeyed his mother and Peter once before, when the old Gate had been his way into Challenrah. He'd only managed to escape notice because the *raffakins* had helped him. He'd thought that was a good thing at the time, but those shadowy sprites had turned out to be dangerous. 'I think I'd better do as I'm told.'

Their walk brought them to the new Gate and Tim felt the pull of Challenrah. Would it hurt to go there right now, with Angela? For once, Madison wasn't around. It would just be him and Angela, like old times. As long as he was back before dark there, time would stand still here. His mum and Peter need never know.

'I can't go by myself. I can't open The Gate,' Angela said. 'Devron always used to send someone to open the old Gate and meet me there. He hasn't "called" me now so there mightn't be anyone near this Gate.'

'Won't Vallend be there?'

'Maybe. But if this new Gate is stable, he won't have to stay near to it all the time.'

'What if I open it for you?' Tim asked, fingering the key in his pocket.

'It won't let me through without you,' Angela said, 'unless I have permission from a Gatekeeper.'

'I'm a Gatekeeper,' Tim boasted.

'I meant a Challendrian Gatekeeper.'

'Oh.' It seemed Tim still had a lot to learn about Gates.

'We can come back each day,' Angela suggested 'When you walk Jasper, we could come past The Gate. If Devron "calls", then I can go through.'

'What if he wants me as well?'

'We'll just have to hope he doesn't, while you're grounded.'

'With my luck, Madison'll get back there before I do,' grumbled Tim.

Resentment began to build up inside him. It wasn't fair. Just because he'd been a bit late. It hadn't even been his fault that he'd still been in Challenrah after dark. If he went back now, with Angela, he'd make sure he was home before he was missed. He took the key out of his pocket.

'What are you doing?' Angela asked.

'Going back,' Tim replied, looking round to check that no one was close by. 'Have you noticed?' he asked. 'It's really busy along here most of the time, but when we wanted to open The Gate, and when we came back, there was no one around.'

'Except for your step-dad,' Angela reminded him.

'Yeah. But he wasn't all that near, and he was looking the other way.'

Tim reached for the padlock and was about to unlock it when his phone rang. He tucked the little key back in his pocket while he answered it.

'I have to go home,' he said.

'What's wrong?' Angela asked.

'My sister's ill. Mum's taken her to the hospital.'

Chapter 10

Cassie

Tim looked down at his baby sister. 'She's so little,' he said. 'Will she be all right?'

Peter put his arm around Tim's shoulders. 'Your mum thinks she'll be fine.'

'I know she fell, but what exactly happened?'

'She was playing in the back garden,' Peter said. He smiled at Tim. 'I'd better get used to calling it the back yard, hadn't I? Anyway, she tried to run to your mum but she fell over before Lil could catch her. She bumped her head on the step.'

'Concussion can be serious,' Tim said worriedly.

'Yes, but she's doing well. They'll keep her in hospital for a few days, to make sure she's recovering properly.'

'Will Mum stay with her?'

Peter nodded. 'It'll be just you and me at home, but we can visit each day.'

Tim ruffled his sister's curly hair. At eighteen months old, she was toddling round the house, exploring everything and often getting in Tim's way. She was talking, too: lots of words now even if she didn't always make much sense. It wasn't right that she should be so quiet and sleepy. She might be a nuisance at times, but Tim wanted her well again and back home.

'Here's your mum,' said Peter as Lil came in with a cup of coffee.

'Is it my fault?' Tim asked.

Lil sat down in the armchair next to Cassie's cot. 'Your fault? Why should it be your fault?'

'I was late back on Saturday and you've been worrying about me since then instead of concentrating on Cassie.'

Lil smiled, although Tim thought it was a very tired smile. 'Of course it's not your fault, Tim. I told you it was an accident. Cassie just tripped and fell.'

It was a relief that he wasn't to blame, and his mum was a brilliant doctor, but... 'She will be all right, won't she?' he asked again.

'Go home, Tim,' his mother said, 'and try not to worry.' She lifted her face to Peter's kiss. 'I'll ring if there's any change.'

'Peter could stay as well,' Tim suggested. 'I'll be fine by myself – or I could go to Angela's. Her mum wouldn't mind.'

'It's a kind thought,' his step-dad said, 'but it's better if just your mum stays. Come on, son. We'd better get home to Jasper.'

After school on the following day, Tim walked along the Strand again with Jasper and Angela.

'How's Cassie?' Angela asked.

'About the same,' Tim said. 'She's no worse, Mum said, but she's not better yet. Peter's taking me in to see her this evening, so I can't be late. Come on!'

'Come on where?'

'I meant Jasper, not you. He finds an interesting sniff and sticks there as if his nose is glued to the spot.' Tim pulled him away and headed towards The Gate. 'I'm going to Challenrah.'

'But you just said you couldn't be late.'

'And I won't be. If it's evening or already dark, I won't stay.'

'But you'll need someone to open The Gate for you to get back.'

'There'll be someone around, won't there? Vallend, or Evrald, or somebody else. The Gate might be stable but there's always a Gatekeeper or a Warden nearby, isn't there? Why are you making this so difficult?'

'I'm not,' Angela protested. 'I want to go back as much as you do but you'll be in real trouble if your step-dad wants you and you're not around. What happens if Cassie gets worse?'

'Don't say that,' Tim snapped. 'Don't even think it! Why d'you think I'm chancing going back anyway?'

'I don't know,' Angela said. 'If you just wait until you're not grounded anymore…'

'Are you going back to Challenrah?' Madison asked. 'Can I come with you?'

'Don't *do* that!' Tim snarled.

'Do what?' Madison asked innocently.

'Sneak up on us. It's creepy.'

Madison grinned. 'It's just too easy. Jasper notices me but you're always too busy chatting.' Her grin faded. 'How's your sister?'

'Still poorly,' Tim answered. 'That's why I'm going.'

The cyclists and the people who had been walking along the Strand were now some distance from The Gate. Tim took out his key and unlocked the padlock.

'It's odd how there's suddenly no one around,' Madison observed.

Tim didn't respond. He lifted the latch, opened The Gate and tugged Jasper through with him. He turned to see that Angela and Madison had followed him. The Gate closed gently behind them.

'At least we're all together this time,' Angela said.

'And back without invitation – again,' said Vallend.

Tim jumped. He'd been so focused on watching The Gate that he hadn't seen the Gatekeeper sitting resting against the thin gatepost.

About to retort that he hadn't known they needed an invitation, Tim thought better of it. Vallend didn't look angry, but neither did he look pleased to see them. It was quite a contrast to the way in which Devron had greeted them.

Tim hesitated. What would Vallend think of his reason for coming back? 'How's this new Gate?' he asked, to give himself time to think what to do next.

Vallend stood up. 'You tell me,' he instructed. 'Devron says you have Gatekeeper talent.'

Tim stared at it. 'It's not glowing…'

'But?' Vallend prompted.

'But it seems all right.'

The Gatekeeper nodded. 'It's stable. Now, what are you doing here?'

Tim looked up at the cloudy sky. Without the orange sun, he couldn't judge the time of day. 'What time is it?' he asked

'We were late back last time and Timoth got into trouble,' Angela explained.

'How unfortunate,' said Vallend. 'It's early evening, and I asked what you were doing here.'

'I need Devron,' Tim said.

Vallend glared at him. 'You what?'

'I need Devron,' Tim repeated.

'Well you're out of luck there,' said Vallend. 'He's busy.'

'With that other Gate?' Madison asked. 'The one that flew?'

'Yes,' said Vallend. 'And that's where I'm going as soon as Grentha arrives to take over here – which should be any time now.'

'How long is it since we were here?' Angela asked.

'A week,' said Vallend. 'Now, I haven't time for all this. You'd better go back. I'll open The Gate for you.'

Much to his embarrassment, Tim felt his eyes burn with tears. 'I really need Devron,' he said. Vallend's gaze seemed to bore into him and Tim wondered if the Gatekeeper was trying to read his thoughts without his permission. For once, he didn't care.

'What's the matter?' the Gatekeeper asked.

'It's my sister,' Tim said. 'Well, she's my half-sister really, but that's beside the point.'

'And what is the point?' Vallend asked.

He sounded less irritated now and Tim found himself telling the Gatekeeper about Cassie's accident and about how worried he was. 'Mum's a really good doctor,' he said. 'A healer, I mean. But she specialises in heart and lung problems, not in children. I thought if Devron came back with me, he could cure Cassie. Or you could come, couldn't you? All Gatekeepers are healers, aren't they? I've got some healing talent here in Challenrah but it's not very strong in my world.'

'I see.' Vallend sat down again and patted the grass near him. Tim, Angela and Madison sat down next to him. 'I'm sorry, Timoth,' the Gatekeeper said, 'but there's not a lot we can do to help you. We need a Deemster to go through to your world before we can have contact there – apart from with you three, obviously.'

'But you already have contact with our world,' Tim said. 'The old Gate was there for generations.'

'Yes, but this is a new Gate,' Vallend explained. 'New circumstances. A Deemster goes through before any other Challendrian, that's Gate law, and right now I don't have anyone suitably qualified.' He held up a hand to stop Tim interrupting again. 'Even if I, or Devron, could go with you, I doubt if our Gifts would work well there. Too much time has passed since our worlds interacted fully.'

Tim stayed silent. He'd pinned his hopes on Devron's healing talent and those hopes had just been dashed. How could he help Cassie now? He stood up and wandered to the bank of the nearby stream. He bent down and dabbled his fingers in the cool water. Jasper pulled forward to paddle at the edge of the stream.

Vallend strolled over to stand near Tim. 'I said there wasn't a lot we could do, Timoth, but I think you'll find your talents *will* help. Every time you come here – with or without invitation! – your Gifts will be strengthened, and they'll carry over to some extent into your world. Come; I have to get you back. I'm due at the village to meet Grentha. She and her team are taking over The Gate here so I can re-join Devron.' He turned away and Tim and Jasper trailed after him back towards The Gate.

A buzzing sound stopped Tim in his tracks. The noise grew louder and he spun round, searching for the cause. Just a couple of metres above the ground, a small, dark mass was flowing along, coming closer and closer. Moments later, Tim saw that the mass was made up of a number of the horrid fly-things with the dangly legs. The little swarm was heading straight for The Gate, and Vallend had his hand on the latch, ready to open it.

Chapter 11

Fly-things

'No!' screamed Tim. He dropped Jasper's leash and sprinted across the grass.

Vallend paused with his hand still on the latch and Tim barrelled into him, knocking him to the ground. Tim landed heavily, almost on top of the Gatekeeper: a bruising fall that knocked the breath from his chest. He lifted his head in time to see the swarm circle The Gate before flying off swiftly to disappear into the distance.

Vallend clambered to his feet and brushed dirt from his clothing. 'What the…?' he began.

'They were trying to get through The Gate,' Tim said. He started to get up but his ribs hurt too much and he sat back down. Jasper bounded around, trying to lick Tim's face.

'What were?' Vallend demanded. 'There was nothing there, lad! Travels here have turned your head!'

Angela knelt by Tim. 'Hush,' she cautioned. 'Don't say any more.'

'But–'

'Be quiet,' Angela hissed. 'We'll talk about it later.'

Tim nodded and tried again to stand up. 'Ow!' he clutched his ribs and settled back on the grass.

Vallend crouched down by him, pushing Jasper aside. Angela stood up and took hold of the anxious dog.

'Hardly surprising you've damaged your ribs,' the Gatekeeper said. 'You could have injured us both badly with that stunt.' He placed his hand on Tim's tee-shirt over the sore spot. 'There?' he asked, and Tim nodded.

A gentle warmth spread through Tim's chest, taking away the pain and causing a slight lethargy. *That's what it must feel like when I heal someone,* he thought, closing his eyes wearily.

'Wake up, lad,' snapped Vallend. 'I'm going in a minute. You can go home or stay here. Your choice.'

Tim scrambled up, relieved to find all the soreness had gone. 'Thanks,' he said. 'Vallend, can you teach me how to open The Gate from this side? We wouldn't need to bother you then.'

'I could, but I won't,' said Vallend. 'I told you I'm in a hurry. I stayed here longer than I'd intended because I sensed you lot near The Gate. Well? Home or here?'

'Home,' said Tim. There was no other option. The sky was already darkening and he couldn't chance being stuck here after dark again.

Vallend touched the padlock and latch, opened The Gate and ushered them through. The Gate closed immediately.

Tim fastened the padlock and stood with Angela and Madison by The Gate, watching as the Strand around them gradually filled with people.

Jasper sat down and whined softly. Angela handed the leash to Tim and he stroked the dog's silky ears.

'There *was* something there,' he said.

'Yes,' agreed Angela.

'What? You saw them?'

'Sort of. I heard a faint noise, a bit like a wasp, and there was a kind of shadowy shape near The Gate just before you knocked Vallend over.'

'I heard that, too,' Madison confirmed. 'And something dark flew off. I couldn't tell what it was, though.'

'It was a swarm of those fly-things,' Tim said, starting off for home. 'They're huge and mean-looking. They've got lots of dangly legs – ten, I think – and they buzz. They're scary. Why can't you see them properly?'

'No idea,' said Angela.

Someone in Challenrah had once told Tim that healing wasn't his only talent, that he had other Gifts that could be developed. He wondered if this ability to see things like the fly-creatures was one of those talents starting to grow. 'If *I* could see them, and you two almost could, why couldn't Vallend?'

'I think he could,' Angela said quietly.

Tim stared at her. 'What?'

'I think he could see them. He was watching something, just before he followed you to the stream.'

'But he almost opened The Gate,' Tim said. 'They could have got through into our world. Why would he do that?' He stopped walking. He hated to think that a Gatekeeper might not be completely trustworthy.

'Maybe he didn't know how fast they were coming,' he suggested. 'Maybe he wanted to get us home and then deal with them.'

'Maybe,' Angela said, stopping alongside him.

'Or maybe not,' added Madison. 'He didn't mention anything about flying creatures, did he?'

'No,' agreed Tim, 'but he was in a hurry. And he *did* help me. My ribs were very sore but he healed them for me. You two couldn't see those things properly. Perhaps he couldn't either.'

'Perhaps,' Angela said.

'Perhaps not,' Madison added.

Jasper tugged at the leash and Tim started walking again. 'When I first saw one of those fly-things, when were in the dog park...'

Madison grimaced. 'You mean one of those things is *here* somewhere?'

Tim couldn't help himself saying, 'Oh, so you believe me now?'

'Yes,' said Angela, and Madison nodded agreement.

'I don't think it's here,' Tim said. 'I thought it was real at the time, but it looked sort of grey and shadowy – a bit like the colour of those *raffakins.*'

'What are *raffakins*?' Madison asked.

'Shadowy sprites that came from Challenrah and caused trouble here,' Angela said. 'They've gone now. Go on, Tim.'

'Well, the fly-thing I saw in Challenrah, when we were by Vallend's Gate, was darker – more solid – and its body was a sort of purply colour. So were those in the swarm by my... er... *our* Gate.'

'So that first one was still in Challenrah but you "saw" it here?'

Tim nodded. 'I guess so.'

'Wow,' said Madison.

Tim grinned. 'Impressive, eh? Ouch!'

'Sorry,' said Angela. 'Didn't mean to bump into you. Your big head just got in my way.'

After school the next day, Tim took Jasper to the dog park again. He unclipped the leash, then sat down and leaned back against the trunk of a tree to watch as Jasper played with two other dogs. One of them had a stick, and Jasper and the third dog were racing around trying to steal it. Tim smiled. Jasper was no longer the cowering, fearful animal he'd rescued from the animal shelter. Since visiting Challenrah, and meeting Larn, the young dog had definitely grown in confidence.

Jasper left his game to dash across the dog park and leap up to greet Angela and Madison. The two girls strolled over to sit by Tim, and Jasper flopped down in the shade beneath the tree.

'How's Cassie?' Angela asked.

'Much better,' Tim said. 'She's coming home tomorrow.'

'Did you heal her?' asked Madison.

Tim shrugged. 'I don't think so, but I might have helped a bit a couple of days ago. Mum went to get some coffee and I was stroking Cassie's hair and telling her I missed her when she opened her eyes and smiled at me.'

'Must have been you, then,' Madison said.

'Hope so,' Tim said, 'but it didn't feel the same as when I've healed someone in Challenrah. It was probably the care she had in the hospital that made her better. Doesn't matter anyway. The main thing is, she's okay and she's coming home.'

Madison leaned over and tickled Jasper's ears. 'Are you still grounded?'

'Nope. Mum and Peter have let me out of jail – for good behaviour.'

'So, are we going back?' Angela asked.

'At the weekend,' Tim said. 'Peter has to go away for work for a couple of days. Mum's got time off to look after Cassie but I want to help. Peter'll be back on Friday evening. I'll tell them I'm spending Saturday at your house. We can go then. Madison, what are you doing?'

Madison had a twig in her hand and was using it to draw a picture in the soil around the base of the tree. She stopped when Tim spoke to her. 'Just doodling,' she said.

'But look what you've drawn!'

Madison looked down, and Angela shuffled closer to investigate the rough sketch.

'Is that…?' Angela began.

Tim nodded. 'How did you know what they looked like, Madison? You said you couldn't see them.'

Madison shuddered. 'It's one of those fly-things, isn't it?'

'Yes. How come you've drawn that?'

'Don't know,' Madison said. 'I like drawing. I was just messing around. I didn't mean to draw anything in particular.'

She sounded shaken, and Tim decided she was telling the truth. She reached out a hand to smooth over the soil and erase the sketch.

'Wait,' Angela ordered.

'But…'

'Just leave it there a minute.' Angela studied the little picture and then said, 'Okay. You can get rid of it now if you want.'

Madison hurriedly scuffed out the picture and threw down the twig. Jasper snatched it up and dashed off to play a new game of chase with one of the other dogs.

'Why did you stop her rubbing it out?' Tim asked.

'I needed to see what a fly-thing looked like,' Angela said.

'I've told you what they're like,' Tim said. 'Big. Purply body. Wings you can almost see through. Dangly legs. Ugh!'

'Yes, and the description helped, but it's easier if I see it in reality, or see a picture.'

'Easier for what?'

'For me to "find" it.'

Tim stared at her. 'You mean you could find one of those things? If we go back, you could actually find one – or the swarm of them.'

'I think so,' Angela replied.

'And why would we want to find them?' Madison asked. 'They're scary. Aren't we better leaving them alone?'

She'd addressed her question to Tim but he was deep in thought and wasn't listening. She nudged him and repeated her query.

'If we can find them,' Tim said at last, 'we can tell Devron and he can get rid of them.'

'But they're from Challenrah,' Madison protested. 'They might be nasty-looking, but we can't expect Devron to kill off creatures from his own world.'

'What if they're *not* native to Challenrah?' Tim said. 'What if they've come in through Vallend's Gate? If they don't belong on Challenrah, they might cause problems, mightn't they?'

'But Devron would know about them, wouldn't he?' Angela said. 'He always knows what comes through.'

'If something or someone comes through a Gate he's guarding or one he's near to, yes,' Tim agreed. 'But he wasn't looking after that Gate until recently, was he? Vallend was guarding it. Devron only went there because Vallend was having problems keeping it shut.'

'So Devron was by our Gate at first?' Madison asked.

'He must have been,' Tim said. 'Remember him telling Carradin he'd left Evrald and his team to look after it? And he said he was sorry he hadn't been here when we first came through. He must have been here as the Gateway and Gate started to form, but then he went off to help Vallend.'

'D'you think Vallend knows?' Madison asked. 'About the fly-things? D'you think he knows they came in through his Gate?'

'He's a Gatekeeper,' Angela said. 'He *must* know.'

'He can't do,' Tim objected. 'A Gatekeeper wouldn't put Challenrah at risk. Anyway, we don't know for sure that the fly-things came through his Gate. And we can't be certain he saw the swarm by *our* Gate.' He tried to sound convincing but doubts kept niggling at him. He stood up and called Jasper to him. 'See you at school tomorrow. Miss Wilson's giving us the morning to work on our projects, isn't she? We'll sort out a time for our Saturday meeting at The Gate. One thing *is* certain: we have to talk to Devron.'

Chapter 12

Madison

Tim handed Jasper's leash to Angela and took the small key from his pocket.

'Where's Madison?' he asked, secretly pleased that he and Angela would have the chance to go back to Challenrah without her.

'Don't know,' Angela replied. 'I texted her twice but she hasn't texted back.'

'She knew what time we were meeting,' Tim said. 'We can't wait for her.'

'S'pose not,' Angela agreed.

Tim paused with the key in the padlock. 'What's wrong?'

'It just seems mean to go without her,' Angela said.

Tim turned the key and loosened the padlock. He tucked the key back in his pocket but left the padlock dangling on the chain, giving the appearance that it was still fastened. He stood back and gazed at The Gate. The chain was around the gatepost on the opposite side from the gate-latch. The chain didn't hold The Gate shut, so there was no obvious connection between the chain with its padlock and the latch that opened The Gate. Nevertheless, The Gate wouldn't open into Challenrah unless the padlock was unlocked.

'Hurry up,' Angela said. 'There are some people coming.'

Tim put his hand on the latch. It wouldn't open.

'Hurry up,' Angela said again.

'I'm trying,' Tim said. 'It's stuck.'

'Stuck? It can't be.'

'It is.' Tim rattled the stubborn latch and tried again to force it open. 'It won't budge.'

'Is the padlock open?'

'Course it is,' Tim snapped. He rattled the latch even harder.

'Hey,' called a man's voice. 'What are you kids doing? You'll have that gate off its hinges! Leave it alone.'

Tim and Angela shot away from The Gate. Jasper cowered behind Angela's legs.

'Sorry, mister,' Tim said. 'We were just playing.'

The man walked up to them. 'Yeah, well. Play without damaging property.' He stopped by The Gate. 'Wondering if it opened, were you?' he asked. 'Never tried it myself, and I've walked past here often enough. Here, let's have a go.'

'No!' said Tim sharply. The padlock was undone. If The Gate opened, it would lead into Challenrah. 'I mean, it's okay thanks. We'll go and play somewhere else.'

The man ignored him and reached out to unlatch The Gate. Tim held his breath.

'Stuck,' said the man. He walked off, looking back over his shoulder to add, 'You kids leave it alone.'

Tim sank down and leaned against the thinner gatepost. Jasper tried to climb onto his knees and lick his face. 'It's okay, boy,' Tim said, taking hold of the leash as Angela passed it to him. 'Just a close call.'

'Lock it,' urged Angela. 'Lock the padlock, Tim, before anyone else comes along.'

Tim shoved Jasper out of the way and scrambled up. He shut the padlock and then, after a hasty glance around, he tried the latch again. It moved easily and The Gate swung open. Tim's breath caught in his throat. 'Didn't expect that,' he muttered.

'It won't lead into Challenrah though, will it?' Angela said.

Tim shook his head. 'It only does that when I've unlocked the padlock, doesn't it?' He pushed gently at the wood and The Gate opened fully, showing the Strand continuing, as anticipated, on the other side. Tim closed it gently. 'Should we try unlocking it again?'

'No,' said Angela. 'There are more people coming. The Gate's kept them away before when we've been through, hasn't it?'

'But we have to tell Devron about the fly-things,' objected Tim.

'We can't if it won't let us through, can we?'

Tim glared at her. 'You're maddening when you're being reasonable.'

Angela shrugged. 'I don't think I can be maddening *and* reasonable at the same time.'

'Yes, you can,' Tim said. 'You–'

Angela interrupted him. 'I think we should go home.'

'I don't want to go home yet,' Tim complained.

'I meant *my* home,' Angela said. 'Maybe Granddad can help us work out why The Gate won't open into Challenrah.'

'Oh,' said Tim. 'That's actually quite a good idea.'

'We'll text Madison again on the way and see if we can find out why she didn't meet us this morning.'

'Must we?' said Tim.

Angela glared at him and stalked off. Tim patted Jasper and then followed her.

Tim shuffled back on the couch in Angela's front room but his feet dangled off the floor. He shuffled to the edge again. Angela's granddad and her mother already knew about the recent visits to Challenrah, and Tim had just told them about the problem with his Gate this morning.

'We really need to tell Devron about the fly-things,' he concluded.

'I'm sure you're right,' David said, 'but there must be a reason The Gate wouldn't let you through. Now, have I got this straight? The chain and padlock are on the opposite gatepost to the latch, so they don't actually hold The Gate shut. You use the latch to open The Gate, but whether or not it opens into Challenrah depends on the padlock, even though it's on the other gatepost.'

Tim nodded. 'The Gate will only let us through into Challenrah once I've unlocked the padlock. Otherwise, it just opens onto the Strand. But this morning I unlocked the padlock and I couldn't move the latch. It refused to budge. When I shut the padlock, the latch worked fine but–'

'–but The Gate only opened onto the Strand, as usual with the padlock shut,' David finished for him.

'Right,' Tim agreed. 'So we couldn't get into Challenrah.'

Jasper rested his head on David's lap and the old man stroked the dog's shiny coat. 'Perhaps there was no one there to meet you,' he suggested. 'No. That can't be it. You went through the first time without any Gatekeeper or Warden nearby, didn't you?'

Tim nodded. 'Devron called it my Gate. He said it settled after I came through. I don't understand why it won't open. We have to get back there.'

David smiled. 'So you said.' He took a sip of his coffee. 'Mmm. That's good. Tea's not the same here, you know. Doesn't taste as nice. The coffee, though…'

'Dad,' said Angela's mother, 'these children haven't come to listen to your opinion on tea and coffee.'

'Indeed they haven't,' David agreed. He took his time drinking more coffee and then said, 'Where's Madison?'

Tim was about to ask why David wanted to know about Madison but Angela spoke first.

'We don't know,' she said. 'I've texted her again but she still hasn't replied.'

'Ah,' said David.

Angela's mum smiled. 'I know that tone,' she declared. 'You have an idea, don't you?'

David grinned. 'Just a thought,' he said. He waved his empty mug. 'More coffee first.'

Angela punched him very gently on the arm. 'Granddad!'

'Oh, very well.' He set down the mug. 'Have you considered the possibility that all three of you need to be there at the same time?'

'Why should that make any difference?' Tim asked.

'It might not. As I said, it's just a thought.'

'You might be right, Granddad,' Angela said. 'For both our visits, Madison was with us, but she wasn't there today.'

Tim had been quite glad that Madison was missing this morning, but he had to admit it could be more than coincidence that The Gate had refused them entry without her. He nibbled a biscuit as he tried to accept the idea that Madison could be an important factor here.

'Tim can see the fly-things,' Angela said thoughtfully, 'and I'm sure I could "find" them. Maybe Madison has another talent that could help in Challenrah.'

Angela's mum held out the plate of biscuits. Tim took another one and gave half to Jasper.

'Perhaps you two had better find Madison,' Angela's mum suggested. 'At least then you'll know whether or not that's the problem with The Gate.'

Tim and Angela stood by Madison's front door.

'You knock,' said Tim. 'She's *your* friend.'

'Don't know what you've got against her,' Angela said, reaching up and rapping on the door.

'Nothing really. It's just…' Tim began.

'Just what?'

'I just thought, going back to Challenrah, it'd be you and me, and then–' He stepped back hastily as Madison's brother opened the door.

'We've come to see Madison,' Angela said. 'Is she home?'

Caleb nodded. 'Yeah. She can't come out, though.'

Tim and Angela stared up at Caleb. He towered over them. Tim took another step back but Angela held her ground.

'Why not?' she asked.

Caleb's sudden grin made him much less intimidating. 'She's grounded, poor kid.'

Tim was about to ask why, but Angela spoke first. 'Can we see her?'

Caleb shrugged. 'Don't see why not. Mom said she couldn't go out; she didn't say she couldn't have visitors. Come on in. Dog, too.' He led the way into the house and pointed to the stairs. 'First door on the right.' He ambled off into one of the downstairs rooms.

Tim, Jasper and Angela raced up the stairs, and Angela knocked on the door labelled "Madison's Abode". Madison opened the door. Her eyes were red and puffy. She took out a tissue and blew her nose.

'Your brother's really tall,' Tim said. 'Can we come in?'

Madison's face lit up. 'Caleb let you in?'

'Obviously,' Tim said.

Madison held the door wide. 'Come on in and visit the prisoner.'

Angela laughed but Tim said crossly, 'Where were you this morning? We couldn't get through into Challenrah because of you.' He plonked himself down on the large beanbag in the corner of the room while Angela sat on the bed.

Jasper tried to climb onto the bed next to Angela but Tim pulled him back. Reluctantly, the dog settled himself down by Tim.

'We don't know it was because of Madison,' Angela pointed out.

'What else could it be?' Tim countered. 'Why are you grounded, Madison?'

Madison shoved aside some books to make room next to Angela and sat cross-legged on the bed. 'My grades were down in Thursday's test. Didn't you notice when Miss Wilson read them out yesterday?'

'No. Too busy listening for my results.'

Madison pulled a face. 'Yeah, well, you were okay, weren't you?' She nudged Angela gently. 'So were you.'

'That's why your Mum grounded you?' Angela asked. 'Why didn't you answer my texts?'

'She took my cell phone,' Madison said. 'I'm supposed to concentrate on studying.'

Angela reached out and picked up a pile of drawings from the bed. 'These are great. Look, Tim.'

She held them out one at a time and Tim had to admit they were really good. Madison had sketched the new Gate, Vallend, Kallyn,

Devron, a temaral, Larn and, most striking of all, Vallend's problem Gate in full flight as it attacked Devron.

'How long did it take you to do all these?' Angela asked.

'That's the trouble,' Madison said. 'I was drawing instead of studying last week so I wasn't ready for the test. Mom was mad with me. Just couldn't help it, though. I *had* to draw them. I'm grounded and I'm not allowed to draw any more until I raise my grades.'

Tim scowled. 'That's not fair. There's only a week of term left and we've no more tests this year. You've got to be able to come out. We can't get into Challenrah because of you.'

Madison sniffed loudly, blew her nose again and tucked away her tissue. 'That's what you said before. Why is it my fault?'

Angela glared at Tim. 'We don't know it is.'

'We couldn't open The Gate,' Tim said. 'I unlocked the padlock but The Gate wouldn't open. When I locked it again, the latch worked and The Gate opened but just onto the Strand. The only thing different was that you weren't there.'

Madison wiped her eyes on the sleeve of her tee-shirt. 'So The Gate wouldn't let you through without me?'

'Looks that way,' he said, ignoring Madison's smug expression.

Madison smiled. 'Good job Miss Wilson's letting me take that test again on Monday then, isn't it? I asked her and she said I could.'

'Monday?' said Tim. 'We've got to wait until Monday to try The Gate again?'

'It's only a couple of days,' Angela pointed out. 'What if Madison hadn't asked to re-take the test? We'd have had to wait until next term.'

'What if her grades don't improve?' Tim countered. 'We might still have to wait until next term!'

'I'm right here,' said Madison, 'but if you want to keep on talking about me, go ahead.'

'Sorry,' Tim and Angela said together.

'Go away,' Madison said. 'I'd rather talk about Challenrah and I'd rather be drawing but I have to study.'

Tim stood up and reached for Jasper's leash. Before he could grab it, the dog dived under the bed and came out with a scrunched-up piece of paper.

'Give,' Tim instructed. Much to his surprise, Jasper let go. Tim flattened out the paper and looked at the drawing. 'What's this one?' he asked Madison. 'Why did you throw it away?'

'It's not finished,' Madison replied. 'It's just a few lines. Don't know what it's meant to be.'

'You must know what you've been drawing,' Tim said.

Madison shrugged. 'I'd just started it when Mom came in. No idea what it was going to be.'

Tim studied the unfinished sketch. 'It's Vallend's Gate,' he said. 'Look. The Gate's partly open.' He passed the paper to Angela.

'So it is,' agreed Angela. 'You have to finish it, Madison. Maybe it'll tell us what's beyond that Gate.'

'Can't,' said Madison. 'I told you – I'm not just grounded, I'm not allowed to do any more drawing until I raise my grades.'

Tim took back the sketch. 'Wow!' he said, dropping the paper as if it was red-hot.

Angela slid off the bed and picked it up. 'What was that for?' she asked.

'Look at it,' Tim said. 'It's changed!'

'Changed?' Madison asked. 'How could it?'

'It *was* just the outline of The Gate,' Tim said, 'but now it's all misty where The Gate's open and there are dark shapes on the other side. It's what I saw when we were near it, with Devron.'

Angela held out the drawing. 'It's just the outline of The Gate, Tim. There's no mist and no shapes.'

Tim looked at the paper. The bare outline of Vallend's Gate was there, but that was all. 'That's odd,' he said. 'Can I keep this?'

'Sure,' Madison replied. 'I'm not allowed to finish it anyway.'

Tim glanced at it once more but the haze and dark shapes had not reappeared. He stuffed the drawing into his pocket.

Chapter 13

Return to Challenrah

Monday evenings on the Strand were usually as busy as the rest of the week, but a quick check around showed Tim that no other people were nearby. Heart thudding, he unlocked the padlock and reached for the latch.

'What if it won't open again?'

'Only one way to find out,' Angela said.

Tim still hesitated. 'What if it's evening there? We won't be able to stay.'

'Get on with it, Tim,' Madison urged. 'I raised my grades and got here, didn't I? Hurry up.'

Tim lifted the latch and The Gate swung open. With Jasper at his side, he led the way through into Challenrah. Angela and Madison followed as fast as they could, just in case The Gate accidentally separated them again.

'Well, that worked,' Madison said.

They had taken only a couple of steps forward when The Gate banged shut behind them, making them all jump.

A young man was standing a few paces away, watching The Gate. 'That's unusual,' he said.

Tim wasn't sure whether the remark referred to him, Jasper and the girls coming into Challenrah or to the noise The Gate had made as it slammed shut.

'The Gate,' the young man said, answering Tim's unspoken question. Tim hastily clouded his thoughts in case this man could "hear" them. 'It's the first time I've seen one do that,' the man continued. 'They can close quickly, of course, but they're usually quiet. I wonder why it did that?'

The man was wearing a dark tunic edged with green braid and with a green, Gate-shaped badge pinned to the left shoulder. He walked up to The Gate, leaving Tim and the others staring after him.

'He's a Warden,' Angela whispered to Madison. 'Green braid and green badge. Senior Wardens have silver braid and badges.'

'Devron's is gold,' Madison whispered back. 'Is that just for Gatekeepers?'

It was the young man who answered. 'Yes,' he said, turning and walking back to them. 'Devron's the only one with a gold circlet, though. He's in charge of all The Gates and Gatekeepers – and all the Wardens.' He looked directly at Tim and smiled. 'He's my uncle.'

Tim gaped. 'Hamett?'

The young man laughed. 'Six years, Timoth. A great deal has changed here. It's good to see you. You too, Anaga. And this must be Madria. I've heard about you from Nashena and Devron.'

It was hard not to stare. Tim had known that Hamett would be about twenty or twenty-one now, but he'd changed so much that neither Tim nor Angela had recognised him. Hamett was almost as tall as Devron and, like his uncle, had dark hair tied back in a ponytail. Devron was clean-shaven but Hamett had a neatly-trimmed beard and moustache.

'Where's Devron?' Tim asked at last.

'He's in the village,' Hamett said.

'Vallend said a Gatekeeper called Grentha would be looking after this Gate,' Angela said as Hamett started to lead them away across the meadow.

'She was, for a short time,' Hamett explained. 'She'll take over again if Devron has to leave.'

'What about Vallend's Gate?' Tim asked.

'It's fairly stable at the moment,' Hamett replied, 'so Vallend's back there guarding it. It still shifts a bit now and then but it hasn't tried to force its way open for the past month.'

'A month?' Madison said. 'It's only just over a week since we were here.'

'I told you time's different here,' Tim said. He glanced up at the cloud-covered sky. 'What time of day is it, Hamett?'

'Just after dawn,' Hamett replied. 'You've plenty of time. It won't take us long to reach the village.'

He cut away from the stream, taking a different route from the one Tim and Jasper had followed on their first visit. Hamett strode ahead, his distance from the others increasing when Tim stopped to take a stone out of his trainer.

'Angela,' Tim called softly. 'Look.'

Angela and Madison stopped to see what had caught Tim's attention.

'What?' Angela asked.

Tim stood up. 'Remember the walk down the hill from the old Gate?' Angela nodded. 'Remember all the wild flowers?'

'Yes, but... Oh.'

'What is it?' Madison asked.

'No flowers,' Angela said. 'Not many, anyway. Look around.'

'Come on,' Tim said. 'We need to catch up with Hamett.'

With Jasper at his heels, he jogged across the field to join Hamett. Once alongside the Warden, all the questions Tim wanted to ask stuck in his throat. The easy friendship between him and the young Hamett had gone. This new, grown-up Hamett was a stranger. Tim dropped back to walk with Angela and Madison.

Kallyn met them at the doorway of the cottage. Hamett waved and walked off towards the centre of the village as Kallyn ushered Tim and the girls inside.

'Come,' she said. 'And that young animal of yours is welcome, too. Devron tells me it's called a dog.'

Jasper wagged his tail enthusiastically and sidled up to Kallyn to be stroked. Kallyn obligingly tickled his ears.

The smell of home-baking wafted from the kitchen. It hadn't been long since Tim's evening meal but his mouth watered.

'It looks almost the same,' he said, trying to take his mind off food. 'The cottage, I mean. How long did it take to re-build it?'

108

'Not too long,' Kallyn said. 'All our neighbours helped – as did the Wardens.' She led the way into the kitchen and set out some refreshments.

'Is Devron here?' Tim mumbled through a mouthful of cake.

Kallyn smiled and offered him another slice. Tim didn't want to appear greedy but the cake was delicious – a moist sponge with some kind of fruit he didn't recognise but which tasted like a cross between a cherry and a peach. He took the cake and tried not to drop crumbs on the kitchen floor. A few fell anyway and Jasper licked them up.

'Devron's with Jeznia,' Kallyn said. 'Nashena's with him. They should be back soon.'

'Is Jeznia's arm bad again?' Tim asked.

Kallyn nodded. 'Devron heals it but it flares up again after a few days.'

'There's something else wrong, isn't there?' Angela said. 'You look worried.'

Kallyn smiled at her. 'You're too perceptive, young Anaga. Devron says it's becoming harder to heal Jeznia.'

'And?' Angela persisted.

'And two other people from the village were stung down by the stream.'

'Are they all right?' Tim asked.

'Regrettably not. Devron was still at Vallend's Gate when it happened and neither of them went to Vallend or Grentha in time.'

Tim felt the blood leave his face, and he saw that Angela looked as pale as he felt. 'They're dead?'

Kallyn nodded. 'I'm afraid so. I expect Devron will welcome your help with Jeznia, Timoth. You can go to him if you like. Her home is just a few doors away.'

Tim nodded. 'We passed it on our way through the village when we were with Vallend.'

'We know where it is,' Angela said.

'I've made biscuits,' Kallyn told them. 'You can take some with you if you're still hungry.' She took some pieces of wrapping that looked like thin paper, folded them around handfuls of biscuits and gave one little parcel each to Tim, Angela and Madison.

Jasper whined pathetically. Kallyn laughed, took another biscuit from the tray and held it out to him. To Tim's astonishment, the dog sat patiently until Kallyn gave him permission to take the biscuit and then he took it gently from her hand.

'How did you do that?' Tim asked. 'He's okay with his main food – he'll sit and wait for that – but he usually snatches treats.'

Kallyn laughed as she washed her hands. 'Here,' she said, wrapping slices of cake and some more biscuits. 'Give these to Jeznia and Devron. And, Anaga, do a favour for me if you please. Make sure Devron eats something. He's been so busy he's been missing meals.'

With Angela in the lead, the small group trooped out of the cottage. Before they had even reached the small gate at the end of the path, Nashena came running towards them, calling out for Kallyn.

'Devron sent me home,' she explained as Kallyn came hurrying out to meet her. 'He's left to go back to Vallend's Gate. Jeznia's gone with him. He wants you to tell Grentha to guard the new Gate again until he gets back.'

'I'll speak with Grentha,' Kallyn said, 'and then I'm going to Devron.'

Tim began to panic. They had to tell Devron about the fly-things. Kallyn could pass on a message, he supposed, but if Angela was able to find the creatures, it would prove his story.

'Can we come with you?' he asked. 'We've something really important to tell Devron. We'll explain on the way, but it really *is* important, Kallyn.'

Kallyn studied the three anxious faces for a moment and then said, 'Very well. Go in with Nashena and pack some more provisions. I'm going to call the temarals. Meet me outside the village.'

As soon as the food and drinks were packed, Nashena led Tim, Angela and Madison out to the edge of the village, taking the route Tim knew well from his previous adventures in Challenrah. At the foot of the steep hill that had led to the old Gate, Kallyn was waiting with Carradin and Hamett. Nearby, there were three huge temarals and a smaller one that ambled straight to Nashena.

'Anaga – ride with Hamett,' Kallyn instructed. 'Madria, with me. Timoth, and that dog of yours, with Carradin.'

Carradin swung him up onto the temaral, passed a wriggling Jasper to him and leapt up onto the animal's back. Tim grabbed hold of the shaggy mane just in time as the temaral took off after the other mounts.

Chapter 14

The Land Beyond The Gate

As Tim and the rest of the group dismounted within sight of Vallend's Gate, Devron, Jeznia and Vallend came strolling towards them.

'I thought that Gate would be causing problems again,' Tim whispered to Angela, 'but they don't look particularly worried, do they?'

The temarals circled the Gatekeepers, temporarily blocking them from Tim's view, then the mounts snorted and raced away. Tim watched them go, then hung back as Jeznia and the two Gatekeepers joined Kallyn, Carradin and Hamett. Madison and Angela started a conversation with Nashena and Tim waited impatiently for Devron to have a free moment. He wondered whether to go and ask what was going on this time but didn't think he'd better interrupt. Listening in to what they were saying couldn't hurt, though, could it? He took a couple of steps nearer.

'Yes, it's stabilised,' Vallend said.

'So why call Devron in?' Carradin asked.

Tim was close enough to notice the brief flash of anger that crossed Vallend's face before the Gatekeeper smiled and said lightly, 'I'm considering sending a Deemster through. Apparently, with this particular Gate, I need to check with our leader before doing so. Well, Devron?'

'I think we need to give it more time,' Devron answered.

Vallend began to protest and it looked to Tim as if the discussion might take a while yet. He hung around – eavesdropping once again – for a couple more minutes and then, frustrated, turned to join Angela. He had taken just a few steps when something hurled itself at his chest and knocked him flat on his back.

'Get off, Larn,' he gasped. 'You're squashing me.'

Camouflaged in the long grass, the huge feline had launched a surprise attack. To Tim's relief, Larn stood to one side straight away and allowed him to clamber to his feet. Jasper barked and danced around until Larn joined in with a chase game.

'Watch out, Jasper,' Tim called. 'He'll squash you too!'

Unconcerned, Jasper dashed madly around Larn until the two of them gave up playing and flopped down together, panting.

Tim brushed dirt off his jeans. 'Very funny!' he said to the girls. 'You wouldn't be laughing like that if Larn kept landing on one of you! I'm going to have a look at The Gate.'

'That's not a good idea,' Angela protested. 'Remember what happened last time we were here?'

'I just heard Vallend say it had stabilised,' Tim told her. 'He said he was thinking of sending a Deemster through. Are you coming?'

'Hadn't we better wait until…' Angela began, but Tim was already heading off.

'Devron,' Nashena shouted. 'Timoth's going near The Gate. Is it safe?'

The Gatekeeper glanced round. 'It's safe enough at the moment,' he called back. 'Just don't go too close, and don't touch it.'

'Come on,' Nashena said to Angela and Madison. 'We'd better catch up to him and tell him what Devron said.'

'He probably heard,' Angela commented, jogging after Nashena. 'Whether or not he'll take any notice is another matter!'

They reached Tim just as he finished a walk around The Gate. 'Looks okay,' he said.

'And you're the expert, are you?' Madison quipped.

Tim felt his cheeks redden. 'Yeah, well – I do know a bit about them.'

Angela stepped forward. 'Devron said not to touch–'

Too late. Tim had placed his hand on the diagonal bar.

The Gate opened. A swirling, rushing wind formed a vortex on the far side and sucked Tim inwards as if he weighed no more than a dry leaf.

Angela, close behind Tim, was drawn in after him. Madison and Nashena, too, were pulled towards the open Gate. They both grabbed at the gateposts but the force was too strong for them. They lost their grip and shot through.

Above the noise of the wind, Tim heard Devron yell and he caught a glimpse of the Gatekeeper sprinting towards The Gate. Jasper and Larn were faster. The two animals sped through the gap a fraction of a second before The Gate slammed shut.

The wind dropped, depositing Tim in an untidy sprawl on soft grass. Jasper pounced on him, licking his face and whining. Tim pushed him away.

'I'm fine, Jasper,' he said, climbing to his feet and brushing loose grass from his clothes.

Close by, Angela, Madison and Nashena scrambled upright. With Larn a pace behind them, they went to join Tim.

'Great job, Tim,' Madison commented. 'Can we go back now?'

Tim tried to act as if he wasn't terrified. 'Sure,' he said. He walked up to The Gate. There was no latch on this side. He walked right around. 'No latch,' he said.

'You didn't use the latch,' Angela pointed out. 'You just touched the wood and The Gate opened.'

'Oh. Right. I did, didn't I? Here goes...' He rested his hand on the wooden bar. Nothing happened.

'Open it, Timoth,' Nashena demanded. 'We need to get home.'

Tim pushed hard against The Gate. It remained stubbornly closed. Angela and the others joined in but no amount of pushing or thumping could persuade it to open.

Defeated and panicky, Tim and the girls sat down near The Gate. Jasper and Larn wandered a short way off, investigating the new scents.

'It's beautiful.' Angela said at last.

Tim turned to her. 'What?'

'Look,' she said. 'The countryside – it's beautiful.'

She was right. Lush grassland dotted with low bushes extended across the undulating landscape far below and all around them. There was no sign of the haze or the dark shapes Tim had seen from Challenrah on their previous visit to Vallend's Gate. The bright green grass was sprinkled with flowers of every different hue and a gentle breeze moved gauzy clouds overhead. Now that they'd stopped talking, they could hear the hum of busy insects flitting amongst the vibrant flowers.

'We're on a hill,' Tim said.

Madison nudged him hard. 'Stating the obvious, *Timoth*.'

Tim glared at her. 'In Challenrah, the land around Vallend's Gate was flat,' he said. 'It's hilly here.'

'So it is,' Madison agreed. 'Sorry.'

'Can't see any houses or people,' Tim said.

Angela stood up and walked over to a patch of orange and pink flowers. Tim and the others followed her.

'They're really bright,' Angela said. 'Look around. All the plants and all the colours. They're like ours but brighter.'

'More so since we've lost most of our flowering plants and crops,' Nashena said, kneeling to look more closely at the huge petals of a tall, orange flower. She reached out to touch the petal but Tim knocked her hand away as a large insect landed in the centre of the flower.

'Watch out,' he cautioned. 'That's one of those fly-things.'

Nashena rose to her feet. 'Fly-things?'

Tim nodded. 'I've seen them before,' he said, 'in Challenrah – but they were bigger. A lot bigger.' He gestured for Angela and Madison to come closer. 'Look. It's got a purplish body, grey wings and lots of legs. It's just a smaller version of the ones I saw.'

'Still looks big for an insect,' Madison said. 'Like the size of a dragonfly.'

'There are tiny insects over there, too,' Nashena said. 'Hundreds of them, on those yellow flowers. Thousands maybe. I think they're what's making that humming sound.'

As if to confirm her belief, a swarm of the minute insects took to the wing and circled around, buzzing softly, before settling on another patch of flowers.

'Those ones are like our bumblebees,' Angela said, 'except they're much smaller.'

'Bumble what?' Nashena asked.

'Bees,' Tim said. 'You have them too, in Challenrah. I remember seeing them when I first came through the old Gate.' Nashena seemed puzzled, and Tim added, 'They're sort of striped – browny-black and yellow, and they're kind of furry to look at. They take nectar from flowers and pollinate them.'

'Oh, those,' Nashena said. 'Brezzers.'

'Buzzers?' said Tim.

'No. Brezzers.'

Tim shrugged. 'Whatever. They still look like bees.'

Madison tapped him on the arm. 'And those fly-things are eating them.'

'She's right,' Angela said, pointing to one of the flowers. 'There were two bee-things on that flower and the fly-thing ate them. I saw it eat them.'

'Good job there are so many bee-things, then,' Madison said.

Tim gave an exaggerated shudder. 'Told you I didn't like those fly-things.' Jasper bounded over to him to be patted and Tim bent to stroke him. 'If those fly-things came through Vallend's Gate into Challenrah, maybe they changed and grew bigger.' He turned to Angela. 'Remember how the *raffakins* changed when they came through to our world? What if the fly-things are eating the bees... er... the brezzers in Challenrah?'

'Vallend would have noticed if something had come through The Gate,' Nashena said. 'He'd have reported it to Devron.'

Tim shrugged. 'Maybe.'

'What do we do now?' Madison asked. 'Shall we try The Gate again?'

'S'pose so,' Tim replied. He led the way to The Gate and tried touching the wood and then pushing as hard as he could. 'Useless,' he declared. 'Let's go and see if we can find somebody from this place. Maybe they'll know how to open it.'

'Not sure that's a good idea,' Nashena said. 'Not every world has people anyway. Mostly there are just creatures or strange shapes and shadows. Whoever or whatever is here, mightn't be friendly. A Gatekeeper won't let a Deemster through a Gate unless he or she feels it's safe on the other side. We don't know if it's safe, do we?'

'Well we're here now,' Tim pointed out, 'and it seems safe enough, but we've got to find a way to get back. Anyone got a better idea?'

'We could just wait here,' Nashena suggested. 'Devron will find a way to open it.'

'Vallend's the one who's been looking after it,' Angela said. 'Maybe he'll know how to open it.'

'Maybe,' Tim said again, wondering why he didn't fully trust Vallend. The man was not only a Gatekeeper, he was Devron's second-in-command. Surely he'd work as hard as Devron to rescue them from this land.

'Let's walk towards that stream down there,' Angela proposed. 'If we can't see any houses or people, we'll come back and wait by The Gate. Look – Larn's already heading down that way.'

'Anyone got anything to eat?' Madison asked as they walked along.

Tim and the others halted. 'That's a thought,' Tim said. 'All the provisions are in Challenrah. If we don't get back soon, we're going to need to find food and water.'

'I'm hungry and thirsty just thinking about it,' Madison grumbled. 'Anyone got any candy?'

'Candy?' queried Nashena.

'Sweet things,' Tim said. 'Like chocolate or sugary lollies.' He turned to Madison. 'Why not just call them "sweets"? I've had to learn a whole load of new words since I came to the States. Lead – leash; sweets – candy; rubbish – garbage; lift – elevator.'

Madison shrugged. 'Not my fault.'

'Pavement – sidewalk,' Tim went on. 'Trainers – sneakers. Still can't get used to that one.'

'This isn't the time for an argument,' Nashena interrupted firmly. 'Anyway, I'm not sure about food but water shouldn't be a problem. Larn's drinking from the stream and he wouldn't touch it if it was harmful.'

'Okay,' Tim said. 'We'll have a drink and then go back to–' he broke off in mid-sentence.

Angela tapped him on the arm. 'What's wrong?' Tim could hardly get the words out. 'The Gate,' he muttered.

'Is it open?' Angela turned to look. 'Oh!'

Fertile grassland stretched out in every direction. There was no sign of The Gate.

Chapter 15

A Bush That Moves

Tim and the girls sat by the stream, watching small blue fish darting amongst the stones and weeds. Jasper lay with his head on Tim's lap. Larn sprawled on the grass a short distance away, with his nose facing up the hill to where The Gate should be.

'Larn will let us know if it comes back,' Nashena said for the third time, as if saying it could make The Gate reappear.

Tim, Angela and Madison remained silent. It was too much to take in. They were stuck in a strange land, with no food, no sign of anyone to help them and no way back to Challenrah. There was nothing any of them could say to make the situation better.

'We could try to find a village or something,' Madison suggested at last.

'It's the "or something" that worries me.' Nashena waved a hand in the general direction of the grassland beyond the wide stream. 'We've no idea what's out there.'

'How about the hill?' Angela said.

'The one without The Gate?' Tim said sourly.

Angela ignored his tone. 'If we go back up, at least it will give us a better view.' She stood up and strode off, with Madison trotting after her.

Nashena scrambled up. 'Are you coming, Timoth?'

Tim shook his head. He watched as the three girls and Larn headed back up the hill. Jasper snuggled closer and Tim stroked his silky ears.

'It's my fault,' he told the dog. 'If I hadn't touched The Gate we wouldn't be stuck here. I nearly made a mess of things last time, Jasper. The rebels wanted me to help them keep the old Gate open and I almost did. I've done it again now, haven't I? Just because I think I can be a Gatekeeper. I don't know enough about Gates, do I?'

Jasper growled.

Tim frowned. 'There's no need to agree with me!'

Jasper lifted his head and growled again. He stood up, hackles raised and lips curled back in a snarl.

'What–?' Tim began.

His didn't have time to finish his sentence. A low thumping shook the ground and Tim leapt to his feet. One of the bushes a short distance away was bouncing up and down. Tim stared in horror as it began to move towards him. As it came nearer, he could see that it wasn't a bush at all but a shaggy, greeny-brown creature with six fat legs that pounded the ground as it stamped closer, picking up speed as it approached.

Too scared even to yell, Tim grabbed Jasper's collar and took the only action he could think of. He waded out into the stream, dragging Jasper with him.

The water was shockingly cold and deeper than he'd expected. Within five strides he was waist deep, with Jasper swimming and trying to bark at the same time. Tim hauled the wet dog into his arms and turned to see if the bush-creature was following. If it didn't mind water, he and Jasper were in real trouble.

The creature halted on the bank of the stream. Balancing on its back four legs, it thudded its front pair up and down on the ground several times. A pointed snout appeared from the foliage-type hair and a long, thick tongue shot out towards Tim. Instinctively, he stepped back. His heel caught on a rock in the stream bed and he tumbled backwards, letting go of Jasper as he fell. The tongue missed him by a couple of centimetres.

Spluttering and shivering, he forced his way upright in time to see Jasper climbing out on the far side of the stream. The bush-thing stomped a few more times then turned towards the hill where The Gate had been. Tim tried to shout a warning but his face muscles were too chilled and no sound came out of his mouth.

The bush-creature took a few lumbering steps forward and then halted suddenly. Tim saw Larn racing down the hillside, mane flapping and huge fangs bared. The bush-thing spun round with surprising agility and took off, with Larn in hot pursuit.

Tim waited until the creature and Larn were out of sight before he splashed his way out of the stream. He tried to whistle Jasper but his lips felt frozen. Even calling the dog was hard; his voice came out in a croak. Jasper took matters into his own paws. He jumped back into the water and doggy-paddled his way back to Tim. A good shake from nose to tail rid the dog of most of the wetness but added to the water soaking Tim.

'Thanks, Jasper,' Tim mumbled through chattering teeth.

Moments later, Angela and the others came running down to the stream's bank.

'What happened?' 'Are you okay?' 'What was that thing?' 'It looked like a bush.' 'Is Jasper all right?' 'I can't see Larn.'

The questions and comments came too fast for Tim to work out who was speaking. He wanted to answer but he was too cold to think straight. He stood there, dripping and shivering.

'You'd better get out of those wet clothes before you catch a chill,' Nashena advised.

Tim found his voice. 'Here? Now? In front of you lot? Not likely!'

Angela's laugh broke the tension. 'The sun's hot,' she said. 'It's much hotter now than when we came through The Gate. You'll soon dry out.'

Tim sniffed and rubbed a hand through his damp hair, dislodging a piece of water-weed. He shook it off onto the ground – and yelped in shock as it wriggled its way back into the stream. He trotted a few paces away from the bank, took off his trainers and flopped down, leaving the girls staring after the peculiar water-weed. Angela was right: the sun *was* hot. His clothes began to steam gently in the heat and he stopped shivering.

'I hope Larn's all right,' Nashena said. 'That bush-thing was really scary.'

'*You* were scared?' Tim muttered. 'How d'you think *I* felt? Did you see its tongue? It nearly got me.' He sat up straight. 'Look, there's Larn.'

Nashena pointed. 'He's got something in his mouth.'

The huge feline padded up to the group and deposited his prize at Tim's feet. Mindful of the wriggling water-weed, Tim drew his soggy trainers away from the object. Whatever it was, it remained motionless.

'It's just a leafy branch,' Madison said. She bent down for a closer look. 'No, it's not. It's sort of furry.'

Tim reached out and pulled gently at Larn's tufted ears. 'It's a bit of that bush-creature.'

Larn spat out a furry leaf then sat on his haunches and began to clean his enormous paws and long whiskers.

'He looks like a giant pussycat,' Madison remarked. Larn favoured her with a withering glance. 'Sorry, Larn,' she said. 'You were very brave.'

'Good job he was here with us,' Tim said, standing up and pouring out the last of the water from his trainers. 'I'll never look at a bush again without wondering if it's one of those things.'

Angela stared out over the surrounding countryside. 'There's an awful lot of bushes. You don't think any of them are creatures as well, do you?'

'Probably,' Tim said grumpily. He was hot now as well as damp. 'Jasper tried to warn me about it. With him and Larn around, we should be okay.'

'Should we wait here or go and see if we can find a village?' Madison asked.

Tim realised they were all waiting for him to make a decision. *Why me?* he wanted to ask. *I have no idea what's the right thing to do.* He'd thought earlier that it would be a good idea to go in search of people but being attacked by a bush had frightened him badly. That tongue had come awfully close. What if they were assailed again by more "bushes" or by some other dangerous monsters? 'Let's stay here,' he said, wondering if he was making the right choice. 'At least there's fresh water – and we're near the hill for when The Gate returns.'

'Perhaps it's moved,' Angela suggested. 'It shifted position in Challenrah, didn't it? It might still be around here somewhere.'

'We'd see it,' Nashena stated. 'It's pretty big – and we could see a long way from that hill. We'd have spotted it from there if it was still nearby.'

'You're a *derralind*, Angela,' Tim said. 'Can't you find it?'

'I can try,' Angela said. She took a pace away and stood for a moment with her eyes closed.

Tim fidgeted. His patience soon ran out. 'Well?'

Angela opened her eyes. 'Can't sense it anywhere,' she said. 'Maybe my Gift doesn't work here.'

'Or maybe The Gate's gone completely,' Madison said.

Tim glared at her. 'Very helpful, *Madria*.'

'Your talent might not work, Anaga,' Nashena said, stepping between Tim and Madison, 'but I'm certain Larn would let us know if it was here somewhere, and he'll let us know when it comes back.'

'*If* it comes back,' Madison muttered.

Tim's stomach took that moment to rumble loudly. 'What?' he said when the others looked at him. 'Can't help it. We've been here ages. I'm hungry.' He pulled on his still damp trainers and went to sit on the bank of the stream, away from the girls.

A couple of small, blue fish swam by. Tim leaned forwards to watch their progress through the reeds growing at the edge of the water. Several more of the little fish appeared, swimming very fast. The first two joined the shoal and they all shot away downstream. A sudden disturbance in the water explained the frantic flight of the blue fish. Swimming rapidly after the shoal was a large, bright-red lizard.

'Look here,' Tim called to the others.

The lizard slowed down and turned its pointed head towards Tim. Abandoning its pursuit of the fish, it thrashed its way to the edge of the stream and scrambled up the bank.

'Whoa! Go away!' Tim yelled, shooting to his feet and backing off.

Angela and the others arrived as the creature lunged for Tim's left foot. Razor-sharp teeth closed on air as Tim leapt backwards. The lizard paused, drew in an enormous, noisy breath, and swelled to three times its former size.

Tim backed off further. 'Wow! Wasn't expecting that!'

'Stand still,' Nashena suggested. 'Maybe it's attracted by movement.'

The lizard swung its head towards her.

'Or by sound,' Angela whispered. 'Stay quiet.'

The creature bobbed its head and waddled forwards, its clawed feet gripping the ground and tearing up tufts of grass.

'It's not going to stop,' Tim said.

He and the others took off, with the lizard chasing after them.

'Larn!' Tim shouted, but the great cat snarled and loped off in the opposite direction.

For a few moments, it looked as if they would outrun the red hunter, then Madison tripped and fell, bringing Angela down with her.

Chapter 16

Dangerous Encounters

Tim and Nashena skidded to a halt.

Tim gave Nashena a shove. 'Run! I'll help them.'

Nashena ignored him and turned towards Madison and Angela. The huge lizard was faster. It sprang towards the girls on the ground – and was brought up short by Jasper's hold on its long tail.

Whipping round, the lizard snapped at Jasper. The dog danced away, still hanging on to the tail. Tim and the others watched in horrified fascination as the tail came away from the lizard's body. Proudly carrying his wriggling prize, Jasper trotted back to the stream and dropped the writhing tail into the water. Trailing red-brown gore, the lizard scuttled after its tail and dived into the stream. Tim ran to Jasper and stood on the bank with the dog as the tail squirmed its way to the end of the lizard's body and re-attached itself. With a sound like a deflating balloon, the lizard exhaled loudly and shrank to its original size. Swishing its newly-healed tail, it swam off and out of sight.

Tim slumped down. Damp tongue hanging out of the side of his mouth, Jasper sat beside him. Tim put both arms around the dog and stayed like that until the girls joined him.

'Are you all right?' Tim asked.

Madison nodded. 'We're fine, but why didn't Larn help us?'

'I can't believe he ran away like that,' Tim said. 'He was so brave when that bush attacked me. If it hadn't been for Jasper this time…'

Nashena pointed. 'He didn't run away. Look.'

Larn bounded up with a huge portion of bush-thing in his mouth. He dropped it at Tim's feet.

'A bush-thing,' Angela said. 'He must have seen it come back – or another one coming – and chased it off. Well done, Larn.'

Tim let go of Jasper and kicked the bush-fur down the bank and into the stream. Water-weeds slithered up from the stream bed and wrapped themselves around the piece of bush-creature. Gurgling, slurping sounds emanated from the twisting mass and within seconds nothing remained of the bush-fur. The water-weeds sank back below the surface, leaving just a trail of bubbles.

'I don't like this place,' Madison said.

Tim stood up. 'Let's see if The Gate's back,' he began. 'We could… Oh dear.'

The girls spun round to see what Tim was staring at.

Angela repeated Tim's words. 'Oh dear.'

Not only was The Gate still missing, but the hill on which it had stood was no longer visible.

'We can't have run that far,' Madison asserted. 'We didn't run that far, did we?'

'Don't think so,' Nashena said, 'but there's a bend in the stream here, isn't there? That must be why we can't see the hill. If we follow the stream back, we should come to the hill.'

'S'pose so,' Tim agreed, setting off with Jasper at his heels and Larn roaming ahead.

They walked for some time before Angela said, 'Where's the hill? It should have been in sight ages ago, and I don't remember seeing these stripy plants before. Have we come the wrong way?'

Nashena halted and looked around. 'It's all different. Where did those trees come from? We didn't see those when we were on the hill. Let's turn back.'

They turned to retrace their steps but stopped almost immediately. The stream they'd been following was no longer close by. They could see the water shimmering at least thirty paces away.

'It's moved,' Madison declared. 'When did it do that? *How* did it do that?'

'And I think we have another problem,' Tim said.

Madison gave him a hard stare. 'Apart from no Gate, no hill, a stream that moves, vicious bushes, dangerous red lizards and deadly water-weeds?'

'And no food,' Nashena added.

Tim reached down and patted Jasper. 'It's going dark,' he said.

Tim was right. The sun had dimmed and a cool breeze had sprung up. Clouds of the tiny, bee-like insects swarmed up from the flower-strewn grassland and flew off towards the trees. A few fly-things fluttered after them, long, dangly legs trailing as they went. Within seconds, the sun had disappeared.

'We'd better find some shelter,' Angela suggested. 'How about the trees? The little bees went there, so maybe it's safe.'

'So did some of those fly-things,' Madison pointed out.

'Not much choice, is there?' Tim tried not to sound sullen but guilt had washed over him again. If only he hadn't touched The Gate.

Larn padded off towards the trees. Tim, Jasper and the others hurried after him, trying not to stumble on the uneven ground. It was becoming harder to see where they were going.

'It's a forest,' Madison said as they drew near. 'There weren't this many trees when we first noticed them. This place is seriously weird. At least the trees'll keep the wind off us. Come on.' She forged ahead, stopping when she came to a small clearing. 'We'd better not go too far in. How about staying here?'

'It'll do,' Tim said. 'We should take turns to keep guard. I'll take first watch.'

Angela pointed upwards. 'There's some light now. There must be a moon.'

'Or two,' Nashena added. 'Look.' Through a gap in the canopy, two bright, creamy moons shed light into the clearing. 'Wake me when you need to sleep, Timoth,' she said. 'I'll take the next watch.'

Larn lay down and the girls huddled close to his huge, warm body. Tim stood nearby, leaning against the smooth trunk of a tall tree. He was tired, hungry and frightened. Resisting the urge to sit down and doze off, he tried to concentrate on the sounds of the forest. He could hear faint squeaks and low rumbles but the noises seemed to be quite far off.

He wondered how long they'd been in this land. Did time pass differently here from that in Challenrah and home? Would Devron find a way to rescue them? Where had The Gate gone? Had it disappeared in Challenrah as well as here? How were they going to get back? *Would* they ever get back? His mind swirled with questions. More and more questions – and no answers. The breeze ruffled the leaves overhead, producing an odd tinkling noise that was almost musical. The sound was soothing and Tim's eyelids drooped. Without meaning to, he slid down to sit with his back against the tree and fell asleep.

A high-pitched, yipping cry jolted him awake and brought a low growl from Jasper. The cry was repeated over and over, gradually fading away.

Tim shuddered and stood up slowly. 'I think it's gone, Jasper,' he whispered. Jasper stood up, hackles raised. 'What's the matter, boy? Oh!'

Standing right in front of him was a figure with glowing, green eyes. The creature stared at Tim and Jasper, and they stared right back, too startled to move.

In the light from the moons, Tim could see the whatever-it-was quite clearly. It was twice his height and looked for all the world as if someone had joined a whole lot of sticks together to make an almost-person shape with two long, spindly legs and four twiggy arms. Its head was as round as a football, with spiky, leaf-like bits sticking out all the way around. It looked far too big and heavy for the creature's thin neck.

'I'm dreaming,' Tim muttered. He blinked hard.

The twiggy-thing blinked back.

Tim raised a hand and rubbed his face.

The twiggy-thing lifted one of its arms and dabbed at its head.

Tim laughed.

The twiggy-thing gave a soft, yipping cry.

Tim's laughter died. What was he doing, exchanging looks and gestures with an unknown creature? There could be seriously large fangs inside that huge head.

As if to confirm Tim's suspicions, the twiggy-thing curled back leathery lips to reveal two rows of pointed teeth. It yipped again and shot out a long, stick-thin arm. Tim yelped and ducked. The twiggy-person reached into the branches above Tim's head and then drew back its arm. Clutched in its peculiar fingers was an object that looked and smelled like a piece of rotting fruit. Relieved that the stick-creature appeared to be vegetarian, Tim stood up straight again. The twiggy-thing hopped back. It shook its fruit-like prize and the fruit-stuff emitted a plaintive mewl as it was forced into the woody, gaping mouth. Yipping in apparent contentment, the twiggy-thing loped off jerkily into the depths of the forest.

Tim felt sick.

'What was that?'

Tim turned at the sound of Angela's voice. The three girls were standing together, with Larn next to them.

Tim stuffed his hands into the pockets of his jeans to hide the fact that they were shaking. 'You saw it?'

'We heard it,' Nashena told him. 'And we saw it run off.'

'Can't have been dangerous, though,' Madison said. 'Larn would have woken us, wouldn't he?'

Tim didn't bother replying.

'Speaking of waking people,' Nashena said, 'why didn't you wake me to take over being on watch? It's nearly light, Timoth.'

Had he slept that long? Tim didn't think so. He'd dozed off, admittedly, but he was sure he hadn't been asleep for very long before the yipping sound had disturbed him. Nashena was right about the light, though. Sun's rays were just beginning to penetrate through the trees.

'Let's get out of here,' Tim said. 'We need to find some food and water.' Without waiting to see if the girls agreed with him, he called to Jasper and headed in what he hoped was the right direction to escape from the forest.

Chapter 17

Madison's Drawings

Tim plodded onwards, each step harder than the last as he pushed his way through shoulder-high grass. Larn skirted around Tim and padded in front, his great paws squashing down the grass and making the going a little easier for the weary group. Even Jasper, normally full of energy, had his ears back and his tail down as he walked close to Tim.

'Poor boy,' Tim said. 'You're hungry, too, aren't you?'

Nashena glanced behind them. 'The forest's gone,' she informed the others.

'Good riddance,' Tim muttered.

'Look over there,' Angela shouted. 'Look, everyone. The stream!'

Larn angled off towards the water and the rest followed. The grass became shorter as they approached the stream. Larn dashed forward and paused briefly on the bank before leaping into the water. He stood there slurping up a drink, his big tongue sending out splashes that sparkled with rainbow colours in the sun's light. Jasper joined him and started to lap thirstily.

Tim and the girls moved upstream from the animals, knelt by the stream's edge and cupped water into their hands.

'That is *so* good,' Madison declared, wiping droplets from her chin.

Angela nodded agreement. 'At least there aren't any water-weeds just here.'

'And the water's really clear,' Nashena added. 'Look at the stream bed. Those red and blue stones are like jewels.'

Tim sat back on his heels. 'Wouldn't touch them if I were you,' he advised. 'Nothing in this land is normal. You don't know what they might turn out to be.'

Their thirst slaked, they sat on the bank of the stream and idly watched the play of light on the rippling water.

'What now?' Angela asked after a while.

Tim shrugged. 'Try to find a village – if there is one here – or try to find our way back to the hill and hope The Gate reappears.'

'I don't think there is a village,' Nashena said. 'I don't think there are any people in this land.' She stood up and brushed her damp hands against her tunic. 'It's just a feeling, but...'

Tim stood up as well. 'A feeling? Angela's... er... Anaga's talents don't seem to work here but yours might. I don't fancy meeting any people here anyway. Especially if they turn out to be as scary as the bush-things, the red lizard and that walking bunch of twigs.'

'So what shall we do?' Nashena asked.

Tim turned away from the girls. *Why me again?* he wondered. *There are four of us here. Why do I have to make the decisions?*

'Let's try and find the hill,' Madison suggested.

Tim turned back and glared at her. A moment ago, he'd resented having to decide their next move; now he resented Madison making the choice before he did.

'And how d'you expect us to find it?' he asked.

'I think it's that way,' Angela said, pointing off to their left.

Tim tried not to sound too hopeful. 'You can sense it? Your Gift's working?'

'Not properly,' Angela replied. 'It's not strong like it is in Challenrah. I couldn't find The Gate, could I? But I think I can find the hill now. It's worth a try, isn't it? The stream goes in the direction we want – at the moment – so we might as well follow it and see what happens.'

Larn and Jasper stayed close by as the group trudged on along the bank of the stream. Sometimes the water flowed smoothly and gently, and they could see blue fish and numerous other tiny creatures darting in and out of reeds and water-weeds. Once or twice there was a splash as the carnivorous weeds snatched something to eat. At times, and for no apparent reason, the current speeded up until the water was rushing by like a river in full flood.

They had just rounded a bend when the water suddenly burst over the bank.

'Look out!' Tim shouted as wriggling water-weeds squirmed towards them through the overflow.

They jumped away, and the water retreated to a safe level, taking most of the weeds with it.

'Tim!' Madison called out, and he turned to see what she wanted.

A piece of water-weed was wrapped around her right ankle. Tim and the others gathered round as Madison sat down on a dry section of bank, well away from the water's edge.

'Get if off me,' Madison begged. 'It hurts!'

Tim was about to tell her to pull it off herself when his healer's instinct took over. Without stopping to think it through, he put his hands over her ankle where the weed had attached itself firmly to her skin. Beneath his hands, the weed grew warm. It wriggled repulsively, turned a brownish shade, and fell off onto the grass.

Tim checked Madison's ankle carefully. 'No puncture wounds,' he declared. 'That's lucky.'

Madison rubbed her ankle. 'Thank you,' she said softly. 'I thought it was going to eat me.'

'There wasn't much of it,' Tim said. 'It might have come off by itself.'

'I don't think so,' Madison said. She rubbed her ankle again.

Tim leaned forward. 'Does it still hurt?'

Madison shook her head. 'No. Just feels a bit tingly.'

'You should be okay,' Tim told her. 'Just let me know if that feeling persists or gets worse.'

'That seems to indicate that our Gifts do work here after all, to some extent anyway,' Nashena said. 'You did really well there, Timoth.'

'So, with any luck, I'm right about where the hill is,' Angela said.

Madison clambered up. 'You probably couldn't find The Gate because it simply wasn't there anymore.'

'Let's just hope it's back again when we find the hill,' Tim said. 'Come on. We don't know how long the days are here. We need to find that hill before it gets dark again.'

Tim brushed his sweaty hands down the side of his jeans as he walked along. What if that water-weed had been poisonous to touch? What if it had turned on him and bitten his fingers? He didn't feel particularly tired, as he had in the past when he'd healed Devron and Hamett, probably because getting rid of the foul weed had taken just a few seconds and he hadn't used much power. *Just reaction to a scare,* he told himself. He did feel very unsettled, though. A mixture of emotions churned inside him: guilt that he'd hesitated when the stuff had attacked Madison; pride that he'd destroyed the weed and helped her; fear that they were never going to get out of this land.

'It's there,' Angela shouted.

Tim and the others looked where she was pointing. Ahead of them was the hill, off to the left of the stream, just as they remembered it. Even the patches of orange flowers were familiar.

Hope surged in all of them, until Nashena said, 'No Gate.'

Not even bothering to climb the hill, they sat down on the stream bank where reeds grew at the edge but the water was clear of the horrid water-weeds.

'We're going to have to find some food soon,' Madison said.

'Don't mention food,' Tim complained. 'You're just making us even more hungry.'

140

'Sorry,' said Madison. She turned away from Tim, took a small notebook and a pencil from her backpack and began sketching.

'What's that you've drawn?' Nashena asked.

'A strawberry,' Madison said. 'It's a juicy red fruit.'

Tim grimaced. 'Why draw food? That only makes it– Oh!'

Angela jumped up. 'What's the matter? Is it a bush-thing?'

Tim shook his head. 'No. Look.' He pointed to a patch of reeds. 'They were just thin and straight a minute ago. Look at them now.'

At the top of each reed was a bulbous fruit: pale grey rather than red but shaped just like the strawberry Madison had drawn.

'That's strange,' murmured Nashena.

'And that's an understatement,' Angela commented.

'Draw another one,' Tim ordered.

Madison obliged, drawing a second strawberry on her page. The reeds trembled slightly and produced a second fruit each.

'Right shape, wrong colour,' Tim said. 'Don't suppose you have any crayons with you?'

Madison scowled at him. She knelt forward and peered at the odd-looking fruit. 'D'you think they're edible?'

Tim thought she seemed remarkably calm considering what was happening. 'One way to find out,' he said, kneeling up and reaching out to pluck one of the grey fruits. He sniffed it. 'Smells like a strawberry,' he reported. 'Feels like one, too. Just looks peculiar.'

He took a tiny nibble. The others waited expectantly.

'What if it's poisonous?' Madison whispered.

'Heard that,' said Tim. 'It tastes pretty much like a strawberry, except that it hasn't got as much flavour as a real one.' He took a slightly bigger bite, then ate the whole berry.

Angela reached out to the reeds.

'Wait,' Tim said sharply. 'It tasted fine but we don't know if it's safe yet. No point in us all being poisoned.'

'Very noble,' said Angela, 'and not at all comforting.'

Larn settled the matter for them. He ambled over to the edge of the stream and sucked a berry off one of the reeds. He swallowed it, sneezed, and sucked off a second berry before padding back to lie by Jasper.

'Okay then,' Tim said. 'I guess we can eat them.' He leaned forward, gathered some berries and passed them to the girls.

'Draw something else,' Angela said through a mouthful of grey strawberry. 'How about some apples?'

Madison sketched some apples and they all watched in amazement as round, grey, apple-shaped fruits grew rapidly on the ends of some more reeds. Tim and Angela picked them and shared them out. A few bites proved they were very similar to real apples except that, like the strawberries, they tasted rather bland.

'Try something else,' Tim suggested. 'How about cheese?'

Madison drew a wedge of cheese. They waited expectantly but nothing happened. The reeds remained still and straight.

'Perhaps it only works with food that grows,' Madison said.

Nashena tapped her on the arm. 'No. Look.'

A small stone on the stream bank was slowly changing to the shape and texture of the cheese wedge.

'Draw some bread,' Tim suggested, before anyone had a chance to try the strange cheese.

'No,' said Angela. 'Draw The Gate.'

Chapter 18

Arrested

'Don't go too close to the top,' Tim advised as they jogged up the hill. 'The Gate kept shifting in Challenrah. We can't be sure where it'll materialise.'

Nashena frowned. 'Materialise?'

'Appear,' Angela explained. 'He watches too many old Star Trek movies.'

'Star what?'

'Forget it,' Tim said. 'I reckon we're near enough. Let's stay here.'

'What if it doesn't come back?' Nashena asked.

Madison sat down and took out her notepad and pencil. 'What if it comes back when I draw it but it still won't open?'

'Then we'll be no worse off than we are now, will we?' Angela said reasonably. 'Go on, Maddie. Try it.'

'Go away,' Madison said as Tim, Angela and Nashena crowded close to look over her shoulder.

The three of them moved back a little and Madison began to draw.

'Nothing's happening,' Nashena said. She started to walk away down the hill.

Angela turned to look where The Gate should be. 'No, wait. There's something there. Look.'

Anxious and excited, they watched as The Gate gradually formed in front of them. It was hazy at first, almost transparent, but it solidified as Madison shaded in the wooden slats.

'Draw it open,' Tim whispered.

Madison rubbed out the line she'd drawn and altered the sketch to show a gap through into Challenrah. The Gate swung open.

Tim grabbed Jasper by the collar and ran forwards. 'Come on!' he urged the others. 'It might close or disappear again. Hurry up!' He paused by the open Gate and shoved Angela, Nashena and then Madison through. Holding Jasper, and with Larn at his heels, he stepped through into Challenrah and The Gate closed behind him. He leaned against it, breathing hard, and then shot forward in case his touch opened it again and that wind-force sucked them all back.

He hadn't known quite what to expect on their return – a welcoming committee perhaps, or worried and relieved Gatekeepers and Wardens – but the sight that met his eyes stopped him in his tracks.

A line of men and women in blue tunics with black braid at the collar and cuffs stood in front of Kallyn and the other Wardens. Vallend was off to one side, next to a tall, thick-set man wearing a tunic like those in the line. Devron, closest to The Gate, was flanked by a man and a woman, both with black-braided, blue tunics and with loaded crossbows levelled at the Gatekeeper's chest. Knives or short swords glinted in the hands of the men and women guarding Kallyn and the Wardens.

The man by Vallend raised his hand in a signal. Two men and three women left the line and surrounded Tim and his friends. Jasper growled and Tim pulled him closer. Larn drew back his lips in a snarl but a soft whistle from Devron brought the great cat swiftly to the Gatekeeper's side. The tall, burly man strode over to Tim's group.

'You lot are all under arrest,' he declared.

Before Tim could protest or question what was happening, he and the girls were hustled away.

The cell was hot and stuffy. Tim sat on the low bed, leaning against the wall and staring at the bars across the window. He seemed to have been stuck in here for an awfully long time. Where was Devron? Surely the Gatekeeper could sort out this mess. What had happened to Angela and Madison and Nashena? Worst of all – where was Jasper? They'd clipped on the dog's leash and led him off somewhere.

Resentment simmered alongside fear. Why had they all been arrested? What had they done wrong? Why was nobody telling him anything? He'd ridden to Vallend's Gate to tell Devron all about the fly-things and then he'd been pulled into that other land where he'd been attacked by a walking bush and an angry, inflatable lizard, not to mention the twiggy-person-thing and carnivorous water-weeds. If this was all the thanks he received for trying to help, he shouldn't have bothered. For the first time in a very long while, he wanted to be home instead of in Challenrah. How long had they been in that other land? What time was it here in Challenrah? Would time have moved on at home? Would his mum and step-dad be worried about him again? He brushed away angry tears.

Footsteps sounded outside and the cell door opened. A tall man in a black-braided, blue tunic walked in.

'On your feet, son,' he said. 'Follow me.'

Tim did as he was told. The man led him out of the small building and down a street towards a larger structure that looked a bit like the town hall near Tim's last home back in England. Too frightened by the guards and by being arrested, Tim had noticed little of his surroundings when he and the girls had been marched away from Vallend's Gate and taken to this nearby village. Looking around now as the guard marched him along, he thought the place was pretty similar to Devron's village, except for the big town-hall-type building ahead.

'Where's Devron?' Tim asked. He'd asked this all the way from The Gate without receiving any answer and didn't really expect a reply now.

'He said he'd be at the courthouse,' the guard said, nodding towards the big building.

Surprised, Tim stopped walking. 'Oh. Can I see him? I need to talk to him. He'll sort all this out.'

'Move on,' the guard instructed, giving Tim a slight shove. 'This is the courthouse. In you go.'

He led the way into a large room. At first, Tim thought the room was empty except for a few guards; then he saw a woman sitting on a raised platform at one end of the room. She was wearing a long, red robe. A red robe! Tim remembered being told that only a High Justice was allowed to wear red. His stomach tied itself in knots. The woman was a High Justice and he was wearing his red football shirt. His hand went to the pendant tucked beneath his tee-shirt. Had it stopped working? Didn't he look like a Challendrian any longer? Could other people see what he was really wearing? Was that why he'd been arrested? There was no sign of Devron or Kallyn, or any of the Wardens. The guard had told him Devron had said he'd be here. Where was he? Why wasn't anyone here to help him?

Before he could ask what was happening, he was ushered up onto the side of the platform and told to stand behind a chest-high metal bar that blocked his way to the woman. He reached up and grabbed hold of the bar, leaning over it as far as he could as Angela, Madison and Nashena were brought onto the platform opposite him. A second bar kept them in place.

The woman raised a hand. 'Timoth, visitor to our land and apprentice to Gatekeeper Devron,' the woman intoned, 'you are charged with passing through a Gate before any Deemster, contrary to the law of our land.'

Tim's head was buzzing. Apprentice to Devron? That sounded good, but the rest of it made little sense. He knew a Deemster was supposed to go and check out a new land first but he hadn't intended to go through Vallend's Gate. That wind-thing had sucked him through. The woman was speaking again and Tim forced his attention back to the courtroom.

'Anaga and Madria, visitors to our land, and Nashena, niece of Gatekeeper Devron and Senior Warden Kallyn, you also passed into a new land before a Deemster. However, since you had the permission of Apprentice Gatekeeper Timoth, and were following his lead, yours is the lesser crime.'

His permission? That made it sound as if he'd planned the whole thing and taken the girls with him deliberately. Scared though he was, Tim's temper flared. The High Justice turned to stare at him and Tim clouded his thoughts hastily. He didn't know whether or not she had magic like the Gatekeepers but he wasn't about to chance her reading his thoughts. Anyway, how did she know he and Angela and Madison were visitors? The pendants made them look as if they fitted in here, didn't they? Devron must have told her, Tim decided. He'd thought Devron was the one person he could really trust – well, maybe Kallyn as well – but obviously he was wrong.

'Anaga and Madria,' the High Justice said, turning back to the girls, 'you must leave Challenrah immediately and for a period of one month.'

That's not good, Tim thought, *but it could be worse. Time's different here. We might only be away for a few days.*

'Nashena, you are forbidden to use your magic or to engage in further training for the same period of one month.'

Tim's thoughts raced. What a fuss. An arrest and a trial before a High Justice just to be sent away or banned from studying magic for a month! They could have done all this without frightening him half to death.

'Timoth,' the woman said, 'you are henceforth banished from Challenrah.'

Tim's knuckles whitened as he gripped the bar. A wave of nausea swept through him as a dreadful idea came to mind. The woman had said he was being banished. Was he going to be sent back through Vallend's Gate into that land with the bush-things? And what did *henceforth* mean? Would he be shut out of Challenrah for a month, or even longer?

'You will be taken to The Gate near Devron's village,' the High Justice continued. Tim almost fainted with relief. At least he was saved the fate of being sent back through Vallend's Gate. 'There you will be sent back to your own land,' the woman declared, 'never to return to Challenrah.'

Chapter 19

Banished

Tim couldn't stop shaking. He stood facing the new Gate, with Vallend's hand on his shoulder. Any second now Vallend would open The Gate and Tim, Angela and Madison would be sent through into their own world. Angela and Madison would only have to stay away for a short time but the High Justice had banished Tim from Challenrah. Banished? Forever? That couldn't be right. How could he make them understand that he hadn't meant to go through Vallend's Gate? Why wouldn't anyone listen to him?

Jasper whined and pressed against Tim's leg. The young dog had been subdued since he and Tim had been reunited just before the long ride back.

'Vallend...' Tim began, but the Gatekeeper was just as uncommunicative as he had been all the way to The Gate.

Before they'd set off, Tim had asked how long they'd been missing. Vallend had said, 'Almost an hour.' After that, he'd refused to enter into any further conversation with Tim or the girls.

The only positive aspect that Tim could find in all that was happening was that it was only just fully dark. They'd been in the world beyond Vallend's Gate for nearly two days but barely an hour had passed in Challenrah. After his arrest he must have spent less time in that cell than he'd thought, and the trial had been quick, followed by a very swift ride back here. He and the girls should be back before anyone began to worry about them.

Vallend placed his hand on the padlock and then on the latch. The Gate opened slowly and with a faint creak that Tim hadn't heard from it before, and instead of opening fully it halted with only a narrow space visible. It was probably his imagination, but was it reluctant see him leave?

Vallend put his hand to the wood but The Gate remained only partly open. The Gatekeeper cursed softly. 'Not another obstinate Gate!' he muttered. 'Still, it's wide enough for you lot. Go. Now.' He gave Tim a gentle shove forward.

'Have courage, Timoth. I'll sort this out.'

Tim swung round at the sound of Devron's voice but only Vallend stood there, along with the two Wardens from his team who'd brought Angela and Madison.

'Go,' Vallend ordered.

There was a buzzing sound and a slight breeze ruffled Tim's hair as he and Jasper and the girls sidled through the gap. The Gate slammed shut behind them, leaving them standing in a dejected group on the almost deserted Strand.

A short time later, Tim sat on the thick rug by David's chair in Angela's front room, with Jasper curled up close to his legs. It reminded him of the time he'd sat on the floor next to Devron's chair in the Gatekeeper's cottage while the Wardens discussed the problems of the old, sabotaged Gate. The reminder hurt and Tim brushed a sleeve across his eyes, hoping that no one had noticed his tears.

Angela's grandfather reached out and patted Tim's shoulder. 'Nothing wrong with tears, Timothy,' he whispered.

Jasper's tail thumped softly on the rug as Angela and Madison came into the room with Angela's mother. Val had brought in pizzas and Tim grasped Jasper's collar to prevent him from stealing any food. Jasper placed his head on Tim's knee and lay staring at the food. Angela gave out plates and Madison helped to hand out slices of pizza.

'Thanks for covering for me,' Tim said through a mouthful of food. A tiny piece of pizza crust fell on the rug and Jasper snatched it up.

'It's a strange thing,' David said, 'but I've felt closer to Challenrah these past few days than I have since I was there all those years ago. I knew you three were on your way home. I sensed it. When your step-dad rang to see if you were still at our house, Tim, I realised it must be dark in Challenrah and time had started to move on here. I told him you'd been about to phone to ask to stay for supper. Luckily, you arrived in time to do just that.'

Madison yawned. 'Sorry,' she said. 'It was a really tough day. It was scary in that other land.'

'Those creatures sound terrifying,' David said. 'You did well to escape unscathed.'

'And being arrested must have been very frightening,' Val said. 'With the long rides there and back as well, no wonder you're all tired out.'

Pizza for supper was a treat but Tim suddenly lost his appetite. He put his slice down on his plate. 'She said I couldn't go back. That High Justice woman. She said I was banished forever.'

David leaned forward. 'You told us you heard Devron. Just before you came back through The Gate. He said he'd sort it out, didn't he?'

Tim nodded. 'I was trying really hard to cloud my thoughts so Vallend couldn't read them but I think Devron can break through that if he wants. I'm sure he "spoke" to me.'

'Patience, then, Timothy,' said David. 'The Gatekeeper will keep his word.'

Tim picked up his pizza slice and ate some more. Jasper gazed pleadingly at him. Tim gave in and handed over another piece of crust.

'Your tale about Madison's drawings and the food in the stream fascinates me,' Val said, handing round more pizza.

Angela stared hard at her mother. 'It's true,' she said. 'It happened.'

'I'm not doubting you,' Val assured her. 'Strange things happen in Challenrah, so why not in this other land? It just worries me to think you chanced eating the stuff.'

'A rare talent you have there, Madison,' David observed. 'Drawing food that actually appeared. Who would have thought it? Still, you told me Devron said your Challendrian name "Madria" means "maker". That suits you well. As for drawing the lost Gate, that was an inspiration.'

'Angela's idea,' Madison admitted. She grinned. 'Tim wanted bread.'

Tim opened his mouth to point out that she hadn't needed to say that about the bread but the others were laughing and he pretended to join in.

'Vallend's Gate didn't disappear on the Challenrah side,' he said after a moment. 'At least, I'm pretty sure it didn't. It was solid enough when we came through and no one said anything about it disappearing.'

'No one said much about anything,' Angela pointed out. 'They just bundled us away.'

David waggled a slice of pizza in Madison's direction. 'This sketching of yours – when what you've drawn actually forms – how reliable is it?'

Madison shrugged. 'It isn't reliable at all. It worked great in the land beyond Vallend's Gate but it's never happened here.'

'What about in Challenrah?'

Madison shook her head. 'I tried it when Nashena and Angela and I were locked up. I tried drawing the cell door open and I tried drawing some food. Nothing. Just stupid, ordinary pictures.'

'Far from stupid, Madison,' David said. 'They're special. I'm not surprised they don't work here, but Challenrah? Well, the magic of that land is still a mystery to me. Who knows what will work there and what won't?'

'David,' Tim said, 'the new Gate. Can I ask you something?'

David nodded. 'Can't guarantee I'll know the answer.'

'The Gate just appeared, but no one seems to question why it's there or where it came from. Why not?'

'Ah,' David replied. 'That I *do* know. A Gate has the ability to make people think it's always been there – and they don't miss it when it

155

disappears, unless they know about its connection to Challenrah. They might notice it's gone, but they certainly won't worry about it.'

Madison yawned again, setting Tim and Angela off too. Even Jasper opened his mouth wide in a doggy yawn.

'Right,' said Val. 'Enough chat. Off to bed with you, Angela. Come on, Tim and Madison. I'm taking you two home.'

With his mind so full of worry and dismay, Tim didn't expect to sleep but he drifted off almost as soon as his head touched the pillow. Sometime before dawn, Jasper's soft snores woke him. He lay still, warm and content, until memory came crashing back, hitting him like a thump to the stomach. Banished. Shut out of Challenrah. Forever.

He blinked back hot tears. It wasn't fair. After all he'd done to help them in the past and after wanting so much to help again, this was how they repaid him. Well, let them get on with it. They could deal with the fly-things without him, and good luck to them. As for Angela and Madison, let them go back to Challenrah – if The Gate would let them through.

The Gate. *His* Gate. Would it really let the girls through without him? He hoped not. Why should they be able to get back when he couldn't? Resentment simmered inside him.

He still had his key, his pendant and his Gatekeeper badge. They hadn't confiscated those. What if he opened The Gate and went back in spite of the ban? For a moment, excitement surged, only to be replaced by hopelessness. The High Justice had spoken. The Wardens and even the Gatekeepers would have to obey the law. He'd be arrested again and they'd probably take away his key, pendant and badge. Worse than that, they might send him out through Vallend's Gate, or one that led to another world, and leave him to die there. Would they be that cruel? Surely not. Devron had said he'd sort everything out. Tim wanted desperately to believe him.

Jasper stirred, stood up and shook, his big ears flapping noisily. Tim rolled onto his side to stroke him and the dog jumped up onto the bed. With Jasper curled beside him, Tim fell asleep again.

His dream this time was confused and scary. One minute he was sitting talking to Devron, the next he was back in the land beyond Vallend's Gate, fleeing for his life from an enormous green bush. A long, stringy piece of water-weed appeared from nowhere and wrapped itself around his ankles, bringing him crashing to the ground. The bush loomed over him and its thick, green tongue slapped across his cheek. He reached up to fight it off and found himself grappling instead with a huge, purple fly-thing that buzzed nastily in his face.

Devron was suddenly there again, walking calmly past as if nothing was wrong. The fly-thing left Tim and zoomed after the Gatekeeper.

'Come,' Devron said to Tim, and led him back through Vallend's Gate and into Challenrah.

The fly-thing followed, swelling to ten times its normal size and joining a cloud of its kind that circled The Gate in a buzzing swarm. Devron seemed unaware of the creatures. Tim tried to shout a warning but it was too late. The fly-things descended on the Gatekeeper, their purple bodies and huge, gauzy wings blocking him from view.

Tim woke sweating and shaking. He clutched Jasper to him, taking comfort in the warm, furry body. The dog licked his hand.

'I *do* care, Jasper,' he admitted. 'I care what happens to Devron and to Challenrah, but I'm not allowed back there. What am I going to do?'

Chapter 20

A Welcome Visitor

Tim walked along the Strand towards The Gate. Jasper trotted alongside him, for once not tugging ahead. It was Tuesday – and over a week since they'd last been here. Jasper enjoyed the freedom of the dog park and Tim had been taking him there each day, deliberately keeping away from the Strand – until this morning.

He wasn't sure why he'd come this way. Knowing he was not allowed back into Challenrah, he didn't want to go anywhere near The Gate. Why had he felt the urge to come here today? He tried to turn back but something drew him onwards.

The walkway was crowded and Tim pulled Jasper closer as they approached The Gate. It was sparkling. Tim halted and stared. It sparkled. There was no other way to describe it. The wood looked for all the world as if it was covered in tiny, shining sequins that were sending sprinkles of golden light out in all directions. Other people walked or jogged by, oblivious to the shining Gate. Jasper yapped excitedly and jumped up to try to catch some of the sparks.

'You see it, too,' Tim whispered to him.

Could it be that The Gate had missed him? Was it so glad to see him that it was putting on a light-show especially for him? Tim took a step nearer – and the lights winked out. Puzzled, he stood gazing at The Gate.

A hand on his shoulder made him cry out in shock.

'My apologies,' said the man standing next to him. 'I didn't mean to scare you.'

Tim looked up at the tall figure and felt his mouth drop open. 'Devron?' he gasped.

The Gatekeeper smiled.

'The Gate,' Tim said. 'That was because of you, wasn't it?'

Devron's smile broadened. 'Apparently so,' he agreed.

'How did you...? Why have you...? What's...? Can I...?' Tim couldn't form the words. He gave up and concentrated on controlling an ecstatic Jasper who was dancing around the Gatekeeper as if Devron was a long-lost friend.

'Come,' said Devron. 'Take me somewhere we can talk.'

Tim hesitated. Where should they go? Not to his house; there was no way he could explain who Devron was. The dog park was too far in the opposite direction and would be busy anyway. There was only one place he could think of – but that would mean sharing Devron and Tim wanted the Gatekeeper all to himself.

Devron waited without speaking and Tim wondered how well the Gatekeeper's talent for telepathy worked on this side of The Gate. Hastily, he tried to cloud his thoughts. He stared up into Devron's eyes and was startled to see they looked deep-brown, with only a hint of their usual, distinctive, orange hue. Even with this change, to Tim the Gatekeeper looked much as he did in Challenrah, except that he was not wearing his gold circlet. His dark hair was tied back in its customary ponytail. His black, loose-fitting trousers, tucked into his calf-high boots, and his black tunic edged with gold braid and with the gold Gatekeeper badge on his left shoulder should have made him stand out amongst the summer-clothed passers-by but no one gave him a second glance. Did he have a magical pendant, like the one Tim wore in Challenrah, or were Devron's powers strong enough to camouflage him on this side of The Gate? There was so much Tim wanted to know.

Devron looked down at him and, quite suddenly, Tim felt mean and selfish. It was amazing that Devron was here. What right had Tim to keep this from Angela and her family? David would be thrilled to meet the Gatekeeper again and Val had never had that chance before. 'We'll go to Angela... er... Anaga's house,' he said.

Devron nodded as if that was the choice he had expected. 'Lead on,' he said.

'Vallend said a Deemster has to be sent through a new Gate first,' Tim said as they walked along, 'but I suppose Gatekeepers can cross if they want, can't they?'

'No,' Devron replied. 'Not usually. Gate laws apply to everyone.'

'Then how...?' Tim began. 'Oh. I remember being told you'd been a Deemster.'

'Yes. For five years before becoming a Gatekeeper.'

161

'Do all Gatekeepers have to be Deemsters first?'

'No, Timoth. Deemsters do have to be Wardens, and also must have certain talents and special training, but they don't often develop Gatekeeper powers.'

'Have you come to find me?' Tim asked. 'Am I allowed back?'

'Yes, and possibly,' Devron answered.

Jasper stopped at a sniff and Tim pulled him away. His heart was pounding. Could he really go back to Challenrah? Devron had said "possibly"; he hadn't said no. 'Why weren't you there?' Tim asked. 'When we were all taken to that court, where were you?'

Devron rested his hand briefly on Tim's shoulder. 'You have my sincere apologies for my absence,' he said. 'There was another emergency at Vallend's Gate. It was trying to force its way open again. It took my whole team quite some time to settle it. I sent Vallend with my written testimony on your behalf, and with my request for the trial to be delayed until I could be there.'

'No one mentioned that,' Tim said sullenly.

'So I learned later,' Devron told him.

'And how did that High Justice lady know we were visitors? How did she find out we'd been through Vallend's Gate? Did you tell her?'

'No. Vallend reported it – as was his duty since he has charge of that Gate.'

Something about the Gatekeeper's expression stopped Tim from pursuing the matter just then. At least he knew now that it wasn't Devron who'd caused them to be arrested. But why hadn't Vallend waited for an explanation before reporting them to the High Justice? It didn't seem fair. Tim walked on in grim silence.

Devron glanced up at the cloudy sky. 'What hour is it?'

Tim looked at his watch. 'Nearly eleven o'clock.'

'Which is?'

Tim's mood lightened and he laughed. It made a pleasant change for him to know more than Devron. 'About an hour before midday. You've never been to our world before, have you?'

'No. The first Gate to your world – the one you helped me close – formed long before I was born. I've travelled to other places as a Deemster but, under normal circumstances, Gatekeepers have to remain in Challenrah.'

'Oh,' said Tim. 'Makes sense, I suppose. There aren't many Gatekeepers, are there? It would be stupid to risk them by letting them go through a new Gate. You never know what might be there.'

'Quite so,' agreed Devron. He grinned. 'I admit I'm glad of this opportunity, in spite of the situation. Exploring worlds is an exciting privilege.' He held up a hand to forestall any more questions. 'Enough for now, Timoth. I need to see young Madria as well as Anaga. You can arrange that?'

Why Madison as well? Tim wondered. He took out his phone and texted first Angela to say he was on his way and then Madison to tell her to meet him at Angela's house straight away. He put "urgent" on both texts but didn't mention Devron. He wanted that to be a surprise.

'Nashena tells me you and the girls are at school together. Why aren't you there today?' Devron asked.

'Summer holidays,' Tim said.

'Holidays?'

'Vacation,' Tim explained. 'End of term. A break from school for a few weeks. How did you expect to find me if you thought I'd be in school?'

Devron shrugged. 'I knew The Gate would draw you to it once I was through into your world. We just met sooner than I'd anticipated.'

Now Tim understood why he had felt the need to come to the Strand today: his Gate had called him. It was an exciting notion. He wanted to continue talking with Devron but the Gatekeeper had become preoccupied with looking around. He didn't seem too concerned by the people but he frowned once or twice as cars and bikes sped past. Considering how noisy and busy this place was compared to Challenrah, Tim thought the Gatekeeper was remaining remarkably calm. Only once did he stop suddenly and wince as a police car sped by with its siren blaring.

They walked on for quite some time without talking until Devron said, 'We're close.'

Tim looked up at him. 'Close?'

'To Anaga's home. We're close, aren't we?'

That answered Tim's question about Devron's powers on this side of The Gate. They obviously worked pretty well.

'Not as well as in Challenrah.'

Tim jumped slightly at the voice in his head and Devron laughed. 'I need to teach you more about communicating with me,' he observed, 'and about setting a barrier so you don't have to work so hard to conceal your private thoughts.'

164

Devron paused and Tim halted next to him. 'What...?' Tim began, but Devron signalled for him to be quiet.

Tim listened for whatever had caught the Gatekeeper's attention but he could only hear the traffic and voices. Whatever it was, Devron was no longer smiling. He set off again and Tim trotted to catch up.

'Why do I always have to sit on the floor when everyone else has a chair?' Tim whispered to Jasper.

If he was honest with himself, he wasn't bothered at all this time. Jasper was a comforting ball of fur curled up against him, and from where he was sitting on the rug in Angela's front room Tim could watch all the others.

Devron was deep in conversation with David. Tim didn't mind that – they were talking about the old Gate and not any current problems. He'd enjoyed seeing the look of amazement and joy on David's face when Devron had walked in. Angela had, as expected, been astounded and thrilled to see the Gatekeeper, and Tim had found it fun watching Angela's mum's reaction. Normally calm and self-assured, Val had been positively flustered when she realised who her visitor was. She'd finally regained her composure enough to sort out food for everyone, although she did keep asking Devron if he liked what she was serving or would he prefer something else.

Devron might be new to this world, but to Tim he looked quite relaxed. Tim remembered how frantic *he* had felt when he'd first visited Challenrah and had then been unable to open The Gate to get home. At least Devron wouldn't have that problem. Tim was certain the new Gate would obey the Gatekeeper when he wanted to return.

Jasper sighed and stretched out with his head across Tim's legs. Tim tried to curb his growing impatience. Devron had refused to explain the reason for his presence until Madison arrived and she was taking ages to get here.

He was reaching for his phone to text her yet again when Devron said, 'Madria is here.'

Seconds later, there was a knock at the front door and Angela hurried to let Madison in.

'What's all the fuss about?' Madison began. 'Oh! Devron? You're here? Really? Wow! What's going on?'

Devron gave her time to settle and then pointed to Tim, Angela and Madison. 'We have a problem,' he said, 'and I have a strong feeling that I'm going to need all three of you. When Vallend sent you back home here through The Gate after the trial, something came with you.'

Chapter 21

Discussions and Plans

'A fly-thing,' Tim said. 'I bet it was a fly-thing.'

Devron looked at him. 'A what?'

Out on the Strand, Devron's eyes had appeared almost human but now the startling orange was back and the Gatekeeper's expression was stern. Tim swallowed hard. For ages, he'd been wanting to tell Devron about the fly-things and now that he had the chance he wasn't sure where to start.

'Tim saw some horrible fly-things in Challenrah,' Angela reported. 'He said he thought they'd tried to get through our new Gate once before.'

Tim nodded agreement. 'And when Vallend sent us back this time, I heard a buzz as we came through The Gate.'

'You didn't tell us that,' Madison said.

Tim didn't reply. He'd been so consumed with anger and grief at being banished that he'd forgotten to tell them about the buzzing sound.

'They buzz?' Devron asked. 'Then that's what I heard on our way here, Timoth.'

Tim recalled Devron stopping and listening, then looking solemn. 'You heard it? With all that traffic around?'

'I heard a sound that troubled me,' Devron said, 'but I'm not familiar with the noises of this land so I couldn't be sure what it was.'

'Show Devron your sketch, Madison,' Angela said.

'You've drawn a fly-thing?' Tim asked, and Madison nodded. 'She always carries that sketch book,' he commented as Madison took out her small pad, turned to the drawing of a fly-thing and handed it to Devron. 'I tried to tell you about them,' he continued as Devron studied the sketch, 'but...'

'Tell me now,' Devron instructed, and Tim related all his sightings of the strange insects.

'So, you saw an image or vision of one here in your world, but the actual creatures in Challenrah?' Devron said, summing up when Tim had finished. 'And they've been near your Gate?'

Tim nodded. 'Yes. And we saw them in the land beyond Vallend's Gate.'

Devron raised an eyebrow. 'You saw them there?'

'Lots of them, but they were much smaller than the ones in Challenrah,' Tim told him.

'Still nasty, though,' Madison said. 'They kept eating those little bees.'

'Nashena has told me about your time in that land, although I'd like to hear more from the three of you later,' Devron said. 'She didn't mention these flying creatures though, so right now I need to know about them.'

David leaned forward in his chair. 'I take it they're not native to Challenrah?'

'Indeed not,' Devron replied. He ran his finger over Madison's drawing. 'I knew from our new Gate's odd behaviour that something had come through into your world. Normally, a Gate won't let any Challendrian person or creature through without a Gatekeeper's permission. Even a defective Gate won't usually let anything pass from our side unless it's deliberately sent through.'

'Like the *raffakins* were sent through the sabotaged Gate,' Tim muttered.

'Quite so,' agreed Devron. 'That's what has had me so concerned. Nothing should have been able to get through the new Gate. I was beginning to think we had rebels on our hands once again but, from what you've just told me, it appears these creatures have come into Challenrah from elsewhere. Apparently, they have the ability to pass through open Gates both into and out of Challenrah, and that's not good.'

'The question is,' said David, 'how are we going to deal with the one that's come through Tim's Gate before it does any harm here?'

Devron turned to Angela. 'Can you "find" it?'

'Could I have the picture, please?' she asked, and Devron passed her the sketch pad. She studied Madison's drawing. 'I'm not sure,' she said. 'I can't find things or people as easily here as I can in Challenrah. I'll try, though.' She handed the pad back to Madison and closed her eyes in concentration. 'I think they're somewhere along the Strand,' she said after what seemed to Tim a very long wait. She opened her eyes again. 'They seem to be fairly near The Gate, but they keep moving so I don't know their exact position.'

'That much information is excellent,' Devron said. 'Well done, *derralind.*' He sat forward in his chair. 'You said "they" were near The Gate, so you think there are several of them?'

'I don't know how many there are,' Angela told him, 'but there's definitely more than one.'

Devron muttered something under his breath that sounded to Tim remarkably like a word he wasn't allowed to use.

'Timoth?' the Gatekeeper said after a moment.

Tim hadn't moved or spoken but he reckoned he must have been "thinking loudly" and Devron had picked up some of his thoughts yet again. He'd had an idea but didn't like it much.

'You know what I'm about to suggest?' he asked Devron.

'No,' Devron said. 'I won't read thoughts without permission, except under extreme circumstances. However, strong feelings come across to me and I do know you have a plan but you're not happy about it.'

'I've dreamed about the fly-things. Nightmares, really. They kept attacking you.'

'Did they indeed? So, you think the ones here will come after me?'

'Yes.'

'Good,' said Devron.

Angela looked horrified. 'Good?' she repeated.

'I can take them back with me,' Devron explained.

Tim grimaced. 'That's what I thought, but you sound as if you're talking about a harmless parcel and not peculiar creatures from a strange world. Won't it be risky? Maddie, what're you doing?'

Her chair was by the rug on which he and Jasper were sitting and he noticed she'd started to add more details to her picture. He knelt up and snatched the sketch pad out of her hands.

'Hey!' she protested, but Tim had taken the drawing across the room to Devron.

'Look,' he said to the Gatekeeper. 'Look what she's drawn! I knew those things were dangerous. You have to keep away from them.'

Madison and Angela crowded round to see what Tim meant. Madison had altered the fly-thing's round body so that it looked more oval, with the rear end finishing in a long, narrow point.

'It's a sting,' Tim declared. 'I bet it was one of those things that stung Jeznia and those other people: the ones that died.'

Devron ran a hand through his hair, dislodging the band that held it back. He re-tied it. 'That's what I've been missing,' he said. 'That's the reason I couldn't heal her properly.'

'Because the fly-things aren't from Challenrah?' Angela guessed.

'Yes. And the sooner I get them out of your world, and out of Challenrah, the better.' He paused to take a drink. Val topped up his glass and he sipped the juice appreciatively. 'What is this?' he asked.

'Apple juice,' Val replied. 'It's from a fruit that grows on trees.'

Devron looked puzzled. 'All trees?'

Val smiled. 'No. Just apple trees – although there are many varieties of those. We also have other types of fruit-bearing trees.'

'This tastes somewhat like our quirrian fruit, but perhaps a little sweeter,' Devron said. 'It's quite refreshing.'

'What are we going to do about the fly-things?' Tim asked.

Devron set down his drink. 'I'm hoping they will find me before any harm is done here. If they're near The Gate, then that's where I need to be. I don't want them to disappear off farther into your land.'

'You look ... disappointed,' David observed. 'Surely it's good that these creatures haven't gone far.'

Devron smiled ruefully. 'It is indeed, but I confess I'd hoped to see more of your world before returning home.'

'You've only been here a couple of hours,' Val said. 'You're welcome to stay longer. Dad and I would be happy to show you around.'

'My thanks for your kind offer,' Devron said. 'Tempting though it is, I have to refuse. These creatures must be removed as soon as possible.' He stood up. 'I'm grateful for your hospitality. It has been good to see you again, Gatekeeper Davrian, and to meet your lovely daughter.'

Tim was pleased to note that he wasn't the only one who blushed at awkward moments; Val's cheeks had gone quite pink. He noticed, too, that Devron had called David "Davrian". Tim had never thought to ask if Angela's grandfather had a Challendrian name. He brought his attention back to Devron.

'With your permission,' the Gatekeeper was saying, 'I'll take the children with me. I give you my word that I will guard them well.'

Devron stood by The Gate, watching as the Strand gradually emptied of people. Obeying the Gatekeeper's instructions, Tim, Jasper, Angela and

Madison waited a few paces away. So far, there was no sign of the fly-things.

'Did your parents mind?' Madison asked Tim.

'Mind me asking to stay over at Angela's? No. Why should they? What about your mum?'

'She just said she hoped I'd have a good time. I've never lied to her before.'

Tim shrugged. 'You couldn't tell her what you were actually doing, could you? Anyway, we should be back in time to really stay at Angela's, then it won't have been a lie.'

He shuffled a little closer to The Gate. He could hardly believe he was going back to Challenrah after all. Would Devron be in trouble for taking him? The Gatekeeper didn't seem unduly worried about that, so Tim had decided to trust him to keep his word that he would sort everything out.

'Why me?' Madison asked quietly. Tim wasn't listening. 'Why me?' she repeated. 'You're the only one who can see the fly-things properly, and Angela can find them. Why does Devron want me to come?'

'Good question,' Tim muttered. 'Ow. Stop it.' Angela had trodden on his toe.

'Could be because The Gate might not let us through without you,' Angela suggested.

'I expect it would, with Devron there,' Tim said. Angela aimed for his foot again. He dodged out of the way before relenting and answering Madison properly. 'I think it has something to do with your drawings. Not sure what, exactly, but I reckon that's the reason. Oh!'

'What's wrong? 'Angela asked. 'I didn't touch you that time.'

Tim pointed to the air above Devron's head. 'Devron!' he shouted. 'They're here. They're here! Look out!'

Devron glanced up then put his hand on The Gate. It swung open immediately. 'Through,' he ordered. 'Move!'

Chapter 22
The Nest

Tim and the others raced through the open Gate, with Devron close behind them. Several huge fly-things buzzed near to Tim's face before zooming away. The Gate slammed shut.

'It keeps doing that,' said the young man standing near The Gate.

'Well met, Hamett,' said Devron. 'Any problems?'

'Nothing new,' Hamett replied, 'but you should have let me go through, Devron. We can't afford to lose you.'

'I appreciate your concern, nephew,' Devron replied, 'but it's my responsibility if something undesirable passes through a Gate.'

'What had gone through?' Hamett asked. 'Did you get it back?'

'They're flying creatures of some sort and, yes, I think so. I'll just make certain.' He turned and placed both hands on The Gate. 'No trace of them in your world now, Timoth,' he said after a moment. 'That's good.'

'Did you see them?' Tim asked. 'They were right there…' He waved a hand in the general direction of The Gate. He looked around and added, 'They've flown away. I can't see them anymore.'

'I heard a faint sound,' Angela said, 'but I didn't see anything.'

'Me neither,' Madison concurred.

Hamett shook his head. 'Didn't see anything,' he said, 'but I heard a buzzing noise.'

Tim turned to the Gatekeeper. 'Devron?'

'I caught a glimpse of them, Timoth.' He frowned. 'You said earlier that you've seen more of these things here.'

'Yes,' Tim responded. 'Swarms of them.'

'If your dreams about them coming after me are right,' Devron mused, 'I wonder why I haven't encountered them before?'

'I must be right,' Tim said. 'Those few followed you out of our world, didn't they?'

'Maybe. Or perhaps they followed you.'

Tim gulped. 'Hadn't thought of that.'

'You need to take care,' Devron warned. 'Let me or a Warden know the instant you see any of those creatures.'

'The Gate,' Hamett said. 'They don't usually slam like that.'

'Indeed they don't,' Devron agreed. 'I think this one has been trying to keep those creatures from flying into Timoth's world, and it slammed then to ensure they couldn't get through again.'

Tim straightened his shoulders proudly. His Gate had been trying to protect them. He glanced up at the sky, pleased to see that the orange sun was just rising. They would be able to have a whole day in Challenrah.

176

Hamett started to walk off toward the village but Devron stayed where he was. Tim was surprised to find he could sense concern flowing from the Gatekeeper even though he looked calm.

For a moment, he considered trying to read Devron's thoughts but he dismissed the notion straight away. Devron had once told Tim he could detect any such intrusion. It wouldn't be a wise thing to do. Instead, Tim asked, 'What's wrong?'

Devron turned to him. 'If you could sense I'm troubled then your Gifts are growing stronger here,' he observed.

Pleased by the comment, and relieved he'd not chanced telepathy just then, Tim repeated, 'What's wrong?'

'Look around,' said Devron, 'and listen. No insects. I mean those of Challenrah, not the intruders. No insects, and not a single flower.'

Back at Devron's cottage, Tim sat on a rug by the Gatekeeper's feet. Leaning against Tim, Jasper stretched out his neck and rested his head on Devron's knee. The Gatekeeper idly stroked the dog's silky ears and Jasper sighed with contentment.

Just like old times, Tim thought. *Me sitting on the ground again.* 'I don't really mind,' he whispered to Jasper.

With Hamett, Nashena, Angela and Madison all present, as well as Devron, Carradin, Jeznia and Evrald, Kallyn had moved the gathering into the garden rather than cramming everyone into the front room of the cottage. A sudden movement near the small back gate caused Carradin and Evrald to jump up. A huge, furry shape leapt the gate. The Wardens laughed and relaxed into their chairs again as Larn padded over to Devron and rubbed his head against the Gatekeeper's shoulder in greeting before nuzzling Jasper and finally settling like an enormous house cat against Tim's legs.

'We have three problems,' Devron declared.

Carradin chuckled. 'Only three? Nothing to worry about, then.'

Devron smiled, then became serious again. 'The fly-creatures, the failing crops and flowers, and Vallend's unstable Gate.'

'In that order?' Evrald asked.

'Not necessarily,' Devron replied.

'They're connected,' Tim said, and went bright red as everyone looked at him. 'Well, they are.'

'Go on,' instructed Devron.

'The fly-things must have come through Vallend's Gate, mustn't they? We saw them in that other land. They've just changed since they got here, like the *raffakins* changed in my world. They've got bigger and nastier. I think they're responsible for the crop failures, too.' He was about to explain further when Evrald interrupted him.

'Let's take your first point, Timoth,' the Warden said. 'Wherever these creatures are from, I find it hard to believe they've come through Vallend's Gate as you suggest. He's a Gatekeeper. He'd know if anything passed through a Gate under his charge.'

'I know that,' Tim said. He wasn't comfortable taking centre stage in the discussion but he wasn't about to back down. 'And I know he's Devron's second-in-command, but they must have come through that Gate.'

Evrald shook his head. 'Surely not. That would mean Vallend knew but didn't report it.'

A soft snore from Larn was the only sound to break the silence that followed Evrald's statement, until Tim said, 'I think he's seen the fly-things, too. Or he's aware of them even if he hasn't seen them clearly.'

'Have a care, youngster,' Evrald cautioned. 'Be very sure of your facts before you accuse a Gatekeeper of something like this.'

Tim clasped his hands together to stop them shaking. What if he was wrong? What if Vallend didn't know anything about the fly-things? He was about to apologise for his outburst but changed his mind. Those creatures *had* come from the world beyond Vallend's Gate, and if Vallend was even half as talented as Devron then he would have sensed something coming through into Challenrah.

'Why?' Kallyn asked. 'Why would he conceal something as important as this? His vows bind him to the land and our people. How could he break them?'

Tim released the breath he hadn't realised he'd been holding. Kallyn believed him – or at least she was considering the possibility that Vallend was at fault here.

'He's never been good at accepting help,' Jeznia said quietly. 'Perhaps he thought he could deal with the problem before anyone found out.'

'That's putting it kindly,' Hamett snapped, standing up and pacing around the lawn. 'The man's ambitious. We all know that. He's not happy being Second, Devron. He wants your position, and admitting to such a catastrophic error wouldn't look too good for him, would it?'

'You've never liked him,' Nashena said to her brother. 'You're biased.'

'Maybe so,' Hamett agreed, 'but I'm also right.'

'Why doesn't Hamett like Vallend?' Angela asked Nashena as Hamett sat down again.

'He opposed Hamett's appointment as a Deemster,' Nashena answered. 'Said he was too young.'

Tim turned to Hamett. 'You're a Deemster? That's why you said Devron should have sent *you* through to our world?'

Hamett nodded. 'I've not been off-world yet, but I'm qualified – in spite of Vallend's disapproval.'

'Enough.' Devron didn't need to raise his voice or repeat himself. All conversations stopped immediately. 'I need to think about this and, obviously, I have to speak with Vallend. We'll discuss later Timoth's claim that the flying creatures have something to do with our crops failing. Call Grentha in again, will you, Hamett? I'd like you and Evrald to stay with her near Timoth's Gate. Nashena, too. Grentha's doing well and The Gate should be fine, but Timoth will be coming with me and it might react a little when he's not near it. I don't want to take any chances.'

Tim buried his head in Larn's thick fur to hide his embarrassing blushing. He really did have a special connection with a Gate. Moreover, he was to go with Devron. How wonderful was that, after expecting to be shut out of Challenrah for ever?

He raised his head as his cheeks cooled. 'What about the ban?' he asked.

'It's under review,' Devron told him. 'I informed the High Justice that I needed to visit your world and that I intended to bring you back with me.'

'And us?' Angela said.

'A month had passed here, Anaga,' Devron replied. 'You were free to return.'

'A month?' Tim echoed. 'If you knew something had escaped into our world, why didn't you come sooner?'

Carradin glared at him. 'Watch your tone, Timoth,'

'It's a fair question,' Devron said. 'I was at Vallend's Gate until a couple of days ago and didn't know there was a problem here. I can tell if any Gate on Challenrah is failing or dangerous, Timoth, but I can only sense or regulate what passes through a particular Gate if I'm in control of it or near to it.' He stood up, dislodging a sleepy Jasper. 'We should go soon. We'll pack provisions and then I'll call the temarals.'

'Are we going to Vallend's Gate?' Tim asked.

'Yes. Anaga and Madria, you'll come as well. Jeznia, if you're up to the ride, I'd like you along with us. I want to keep a check on that arm. Between us, Timoth and I should be able to hold the infection at bay. Carradin, accompany us, please.' Devron turned to Kallyn. 'You too, if you will, Kallyn, and before you reprimand me for taking the children, I know it might be risky but I'm certain we're going to need their help at some point.'

Larn chose that moment to stand up and shake, his shaggy mane sending fine hairs over Tim's clothing. Tim brushed them off and Larn settled down by him again.

'Timoth,' Devron said, 'before we go, tell me more about the fly-creatures and why you believe they are connected to the failure of our crops.'

'I've just done a project on ecology, with Anaga and Madria – for school,' Tim said.

'Ecology?'

'It's how things work together in the natural world. How they need each other.'

'And?' Devron prompted.

'We wanted to study bees, because some of the chemicals people have used to help keep our crops free from pests have killed off an awful lot of our bees.'

'Chemicals?'

'Poisonous stuff,' Tim explained.

Devron frowned. 'Your people use poisons on crops?'

'Yes,' Tim confirmed. 'Except for organic farmers. They use natural materials.'

'And I take it that bees are not pests?'

'No. They're useful. They pollinate plants and some of them make honey. That's a kind of sugary stuff that's good to eat. Anyway, if we lose our bees, we'll lose our crops because the crops need pollinating.'

Devron nodded his understanding. 'Your bees must be like our brezzers.'

'They are,' Tim agreed. 'They even look very similar.'

'At Anaga's house, Madria mentioned that your fly-creatures in the place beyond Vallend's Gate were eating bees.'

'Yes. I think the fly-things have come into Challenrah and have grown much larger here,' Tim continued. 'I bet they've been eating your brezzers, and those are the pollinators, aren't they?'

'They're our main pollinators, yes. Their loss would explain the crop failures and the loss of flowering plants.'

'That's what I thought,' Tim said. 'We have to get rid of them, don't we?'

'We have to find them first,' Devron said, 'and then work out a way of opening Vallend's Gate safely and enticing the creatures back to where they belong.'

Tim gave a sigh of relief. At last he'd managed to convince Devron that the horrid fly-things had come in through Vallend's Gate.

'The fields around the old barn to the north of the village,' Jeznia said. 'They were the first to be affected.'

'You think these creatures might have settled somewhere near there?' Devron guessed.

Jeznia rubbed gently at her injured arm. 'It's possible, isn't it? I wanted young Timoth to take a look at those fields with me when he first came back to Challenrah. I thought he might be able to sense what was wrong with the crops there, but we didn't have the chance.'

'Then we'll go now,' Devron decided. 'We should still be able to reach Vallend's Gate by mid-morning if we don't linger at the fields. Kallyn, I'll leave Madria in your care for the time being. Jeznia, too. I don't want her walking and then riding.'

'I'll prepare the provisions for the ride to Vallend's Gate,' Kallyn said. 'Come, Madria; you can help me. Jeznia – stay where you are and rest while you can.'

Ignoring Jeznia's protests, Kallyn headed indoors with Madison while Devron led the way out of the garden and towards the northern fields.

The walk took them part of the way to the site of the old Gate that had caused so many problems in the past. Recalling how he had been kidnapped by the rebels, leaving Hamett injured on the hillside, Tim was quite thankful when Devron turned aside and guided the group off in a different direction. Moments later, the three great leodans joined them.

Tim smiled as he walked along with Devron and the Wardens and the big felines, and with just Angela and Nashena – and Jasper, of course. 'No Madison,' he whispered to the young dog. 'Good, isn't it?'

Why do I resent Madison tagging along? he wondered. *She's not that bad really, and if it hadn't been for her drawing of Vallend's Gate, we'd still be stuck in that other land.* Perhaps he should make more effort to be kinder to her. Still, it felt like old times to be without her. He might as well enjoy it while it lasted.

'Over there,' said Devron, and Tim spotted a ramshackle building which he assumed must be the old barn Jeznia had mentioned. 'Keep alert,' the Gatekeeper cautioned. 'If those creatures *are* around here, they're probably dangerous. Anaga, can you tell if there are any nearby?'

'I can't sense any,' Angela reported. 'There's just a very faint trace of them but, as far as I can tell, they're not here at the moment.'

Tim's head swam with a sudden wave of dizziness. Right in front of him, he could see timber walls and beams, and a huge conical nest dangling from the wooden ceiling. Fly-things were buzzing in and out of the nest: lots of them; too many to count.

Chapter 23

Lessons and Lies

Tim took a wobbly step back and Devron caught him by the arm to steady him. The vision of the fly-things faded and the dizziness passed swiftly.

'What's wrong?' the Gatekeeper asked.

'The barn,' Tim said. 'That's their base here.'

'The barn?' Devron repeated. 'Anaga, are you sure they're not in there at present?'

Angela nodded. 'Definitely not,' she confirmed.

'They were flying in and out,' Tim said. 'I saw something that looked a bit like a gigantic wasps' nest. Well, I didn't actually see it, but it came into my mind and I thought it was really there.'

'Wasps?' Devron queried.

Tim noticed the Gatekeeper didn't question his vision, just the word he'd used. 'They're small, flying insects that have a nasty sting,' he explained. 'They make a kind of papery nest.'

Without further conversation, Devron headed straight for the old barn. The rest of the group followed quickly.

Tim was right. High in the corner, where the beams were still fairly solid, there was a massive, greeny-brown, papery construction that gave off a slightly sour smell. Larn and Jasper sneezed at the same time and backed out of the barn to go and stand with Parrin and Syeesha. Devron walked closer to the nest. He reached out and held his hand beneath the structure, taking care not to touch it.

'I have a clear idea of what they look like now,' he said, lowering his hand. 'Madria's drawing helped a great deal, but now I know the colours.' He turned to face the others. 'Good work, Timoth. This has obviously been their home, and that would explain why the first crop failures were in this area. Anaga's correct, though. They're not here, so the question is: where are they?'

'What should we do now?' Hamett asked. 'There's no telling where these creatures have gone.'

'True,' agreed Devron, 'and I can't wait here on the chance they'll return soon. I have to check Vallend's Gate, and speak with him about these creatures.'

'If they *are* drawn to you, or to me,' Tim said, 'then maybe they'll come to find us at Vallend's Gate. We want them there anyway, don't we?'

'Another good reason to ride there immediately,' Devron said. 'Hamett and Evrald – and you, too, Nashena – once Grentha has control of Timoth's Gate, keep checking back here and "contact" me if the creatures return. You might not be able to see them clearly but you should be able to detect some sign of them. Take care. I don't want anyone else to suffer a sting.'

Carradin stepped forward with a rotting plank in his hand. 'I'll get rid of that nest.'

Devron stopped him. 'When I was close to the nest, I sensed not only what they looked like, but what might happen if they remain in Challenrah.'

Carradin lowered the plank. 'Go on.'

'If they breed and spread across the land, we'll have many more deaths from their stings, and our brezzers will be wiped out. I'm loathe to destroy any creature, but if we can't lure them out of Challenrah and back to their own land, they'll doubtless return to this nest. Since I know this is their base, I'll be able come back here to take the necessary measures.' He glanced once more at the nest and then strode out of the barn.

Tim had grown used to the strange appearance of the temarals but he still found their speed unnerving. Parrin, Syeesha and Larn had no trouble keeping pace, though. They raced alongside the temarals, giving every appearance of enjoying the run.

Kallyn, Jeznia and Madison had joined them again, and Tim was riding with Jeznia (so he could sense if the Warden became ill again, Devron had said). Tim clasped Jasper to him with one arm and held tightly to the temaral's mane with the other hand. He wasn't sure whether to be glad or sorry when the mounts slowed to a rolling walk and halted with Vallend's Gate in sight. There were three people sitting on the grass near The Gate: Vallend, and two Wardens with green-braided tunics.

Devron walked off towards The Gate, calling back, 'Wait here, everyone.'

Tim saw Vallend and the other two people stand as Devron approached with Parrin and Syeesha at his heels. Larn stayed with Tim and Jasper. Vallend took a few steps forward to meet Devron. Tim tried to hear what was said but he was too far away. He was about to try "listening" telepathically when Devron turned and came back. Deciding the idea hadn't been sensible, Tim attempted to look innocent.

'Well?' Kallyn asked before Tim could say anything.

Devron shrugged. 'He knows nothing about the creatures.'

'He didn't know why your message hadn't reached High Justice Rellia, either,' Kallyn reminded her husband.

Devron nodded. 'So he said.'

Tim was about to comment but Kallyn spoke first, stating just what Tim had been going to say. 'You don't believe him. I can tell by your expression.'

Devron smiled. 'It's fortunate Vallend doesn't know me as well as you do.'

'All Gatekeepers are telepathic, aren't they?' Tim asked.

'Yes,' Devron answered. 'To a greater or lesser degree. Wardens, too. Why?'

'I know *you* can shield what *you're* thinking,' Tim explained, 'and I know you told me people don't usually "read" other people's thoughts without permission, but...'

'But what?' Devron prompted.

'What if Vallend can break through my cloud and "read" what I'm thinking?'

Devron appeared to consider Tim's fear. 'I wish I had more time to teach you,' he said. 'One of these days, perhaps you'll come to Challenrah when there *isn't* a crisis!' He frowned thoughtfully. 'There is one safety measure we can take. Come with me. Kallyn, will you and the others sort refreshments, please? For Vallend and his Wardens as well.'

'Yes, of course,' Kallyn said, 'and don't look at me like that. I won't let Vallend know what I really think of him!'

Devron chuckled as he led Tim a short distance away from the group. 'Sit,' he said, and laughed as Jasper sat down, tongue lolling from the side of his mouth as if he was grinning.

Tim patted the young dog and sat by him on the grass. Devron knelt in front of them.

'Your own shield is strong,' Devron told Tim. 'Keep practising and it will become second-nature to you. Eventually, you'll set up the barrier without conscious decision. It will be there unless you lower it deliberately. For now, I want you to set your defence.'

Tim reached for his thick, fluffy cloud and wrapped it around his thoughts. He'd just sealed it like a tucked-in blanket when he felt a pressure in his head. It wasn't painful but it was most uncomfortable. He let the cloud disperse and the pressure went away.

I take it from your reaction that you felt that, said Devron in Tim's mind.

'Yes,' Tim replied. Devron raised an eyebrow and Tim changed to thought-speech. *Yes.*

Good. But you let go of your barrier. Don't do that. Strengthen it if you feel something pushing against it. Try again.

Tim did as he was told. It took him several attempts before he could hold on to his cloud when Devron pressed against it.

Devron nodded approval. *Better. We'll practise this whenever we have time. Kallyn's adept, too, so you can also try this with her. Now, release your shield.*

Tim let the cloud thin and fade away. He blinked hard, feeling surprisingly tired. Thought-control lessons were more taxing than he'd expected. *I...* he began. A sudden giddiness made him feel momentarily light-headed. 'Oh! What was that?'

'That, Timoth,' said Devron, speaking aloud as Tim had done, 'shows me you'll be able to tell if someone tries to read your thoughts when you are not shielding them. Well done for noticing it. Cloud your thoughts immediately if ever you feel that sensation.'

Tim beamed at the praise. 'I still believe you could do it without me knowing or feeling anything if you really wanted to,' he said.

'I could,' Devron admitted, 'but it's not something I'd want to do. Fortunately for everyone, there are very few telepaths who can break through a well-set barrier without alerting the person they're trying to "read".'

'Can Vallend?' Tim asked quietly.

Devron shook his head. 'No.'

'Good,' Tim said, rubbing his forehead.

Devron stood up. 'Come. You'll feel better when you've eaten.'

Jasper seemed to understand that idea. He dashed ahead of Tim and Devron, and sat with his tail waving, staring pleadingly at Kallyn until she gave him some cheese.

Tim sat with Angela and Madison on the red-tinted grass a short way off from the adults. 'They're chatting with Vallend and his Wardens as if there's nothing wrong,' he said.

'Devron knows what he's doing,' Angela responded. 'He can't want Vallend to know he suspects him of lying.'

Tim plucked a long stem of grass and chewed it thoughtfully. 'He doesn't just suspect him. He knows full well he's lying. Why doesn't he come right out and say so?'

'Maybe he wants to give Vallend a chance to own up,' Angela suggested.

Tim spat out the grass and ate some bread and cheese instead. Jasper nudged his arm and Tim gave him a small piece of cheese. Something brushed the back of his neck and he spun round expecting Larn to have crept up on him in his usual, mischievous manner. The leodan wasn't there.

'Where's Larn?' he asked.

Angela pointed. 'Over by Devron and Kallyn.'

Tim sat perfectly still and listened intently. In addition to the adults' voices, he could hear a faint buzzing. His hands went clammy and his stomach began to churn.

'You've gone white,' Angela said in concern. 'What's the matter?'

Tim dropped the rest of his cheese and stood up quickly. Jasper snatched up the tasty morsel and bounded after him as he ran towards Devron.

The Gatekeeper rose quickly and held up his hand to stop Tim in his tracks. *Walk!* he ordered in Tim's head. *If there's something you need to tell me, do so without showing such concern.*

Tim tried his best to look calm. *I think they're on their way here, Devron,* he "said". *The fly-things. I think they're coming.*

Chapter 24

Back Through Vallend's Gate

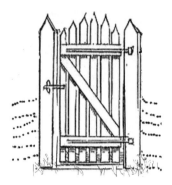

'Is there a problem?' Vallend asked as Tim and Angela joined the group.

'Possibly,' Devron replied. 'Those flying creatures I mentioned...'

'The ones that have mysteriously appeared and can only be seen by young Timoth?'

Tim clamped his jaws tightly to stop himself from answering Vallend back. For good measure, he clouded his thoughts.

'And by the way,' Vallend said to Devron, 'you've not yet told me why this young man is back here when he's been banished.'

'He's here because I brought him,' Devron replied. 'His sentence is under review. As for the invading creatures, it's not just Timoth who's certain they're here. He's been able to see them properly for a while, but I caught a glimpse of them when we drew them back from his world, and that nest I told you about gave me a clear image of them – and a very good idea of the disaster they'll cause if they remain in Challenrah.'

Vallend put down his drink and stood up. 'Well then, it they *are* here, we need to get rid of them before they do any harm.'

'It's a bit late for that,' Jeznia said. 'We believe it was one of them that stung me and the two villagers who died – and we think they've been devouring our brezzers.'

Vallend looked genuinely shocked. 'You think their stings caused the deaths of those people? And they're killing brezzers? If that's true, it would explain the crop failures.'

'Quite so,' said Devron.

Vallend scratched at his close-trimmed beard. 'So, where have they come from?'

Devron gestured to The Gate. 'Timoth and the girls saw such creatures in the land beyond this Gate.'

'You're not suggesting they came through?'

'It seems the only explanation of their presence,' Devron said.

'I'd have known,' Vallend declared.

'Yes,' agreed Devron mildly, 'but we can discuss that later. Right now, my priority is to get the creatures out of Challenrah and back to where they belong. Timoth thinks they're around here somewhere. They could be deadly to us as well as our brezzers. We've already lost a couple of people to their stings, and Jeznia's still suffering the effects.'

'I take it you have a plan of some sort,' Vallend said. 'How can I help?'

Tim nudged Angela. 'He sounds so sincere,' he whispered. He took a step closer to Devron as Kallyn and the other Wardens gathered round.

'We need a controlled, partial opening of The Gate,' Devron said. 'We can't allow more creatures to come through but we have to open it sufficiently to lead the ones here back to their land.'

Vallend shook his head. 'A *controlled* opening? That's not going to be easy. You know how hard it's been to keep it closed. It really wants to be fully open. It'll fight us all the way. Added to which, it might not stay still. And what if you're sending these creatures to a land where they don't belong?'

Devron ignored Vallend's last query. 'With your Wardens and mine, can you keep it in place and stop it opening fully?' he asked.

Vallend shrugged. 'Possibly. What will you be doing? We'd stand more chance if you took charge here.'

'What an admission,' Carradin mumbled under his breath.

Tim heard him and grinned.

'If it works as it did from Timoth's world back to Challenrah,' Devron said, 'I'll be going through The Gate with the creatures after me.'

Kallyn's sharp intake of breath gave away the fact that Devron hadn't told her what he had in mind. Tim had guessed, though, but he knew with a horrid, sinking realisation that it couldn't just be Devron. They didn't know whether the fly-things were drawn to the Gatekeeper or to Tim so, as far as Tim could see, both he and Devron would have to wait together until the fly-things were close by and then dash through The Gate and hope the creatures followed.

Sure enough, Devron saying, 'Here's the part you're not going to like, Kallyn: Timoth will have to be with me – I believe he's already worked that out – and so will Anaga and Madria.'

'I'm not happy with you taking that chance yourself,' Kallyn said, 'but I certainly don't think the children should be involved.'

'I don't like the idea any more than you do,' Devron confessed, 'but I strongly suspect The Gate will disappear when we're through, as it did for the children. I can find any Gate on Challenrah but I rather think I'll need Anaga to find its position in that other land, and Madria to sketch it back into existence.'

Tim rubbed his forehead again. He'd felt quite all right after having some food but now he was queasy and his head had started to ache. *It's just nerves,* he told himself. The very idea of going back into that strange land was enough to make anyone scared.

Devron called Angela and Madison to him. 'This could be dangerous,' he said. 'You two and Timoth have already experienced the world beyond this Gate. You are well within your rights to refuse to go there again. No one will think any less of you if you decide not to chance it. It's – possible – I'll be able to open The Gate from the other side and your presence won't be needed anyway.'

'You said you suspect The Gate will disappear, like it did before,' Angela said, 'and that you mightn't be able to find it.'

Devron shrugged. 'I could be wrong.'

'When have you been wrong about something to do with a Gate?' Tim asked.

'Never,' murmured Carradin.

'That's what I thought,' Tim said.

'So you'd be stuck there,' Madison declared.

Tim looked questioningly at Angela and Madison and they both nodded. *Surely we'll be safe as long as we're with Devron,* Tim thought. 'We're all going with you,' he announced.

Walking with Devron towards The Gate, Tim wondered if the girls were as terrified as he was. He had no chance to ask them. A furious buzzing assaulted his ears as a huge swarm of fly-things circled The Gate. He wanted to scream a warning but his throat seemed to have closed up. He resorted to telepathy.

They're here, Devron! They're all round The Gate!

The Gatekeeper glanced up. *I see them, Timoth.* 'Now, Vallend!' he shouted. 'I'll release it. You and the Wardens control it. *Don't* let it open fully!'

The Gate shuddered. The gateposts held firm but the wooden slats in between them twisted and writhed as if they were alive. The latch rattled furiously and the low fence jigged up and down in a wave-like motion. The movement made Tim feel even more sick.

They were near The Gate now, with Tim and Devron a few paces ahead of the girls. Jasper had ignored Tim's "stay" instruction and he pressed against Tim's legs, almost tripping him up. The leodans tried to follow but Devron sent them back. Syeesha and Parrin obeyed, but Larn sneaked after Tim and Jasper.

'Stay close, Timoth,' Devron ordered. 'I might be able to shield us.'

The Gate steadied when Devron placed his hand on the diagonal plank. The fly-things abandoned their circling and zoomed towards Tim and Devron. *Him or me?* Tim wondered, trying not to give in to panic. As if in answer to his unspoken question, all but one of the fly-things changed direction at the last second and descended in a buzzing mass upon the Gatekeeper.

Before Tim could react, The Gate opened and for an instant Tim saw the misty barrier and the dark shapes swirling within it. The single fly-thing landed on his hand and he stepped back in shock. Then the mist vanished and the windy vortex snatched him and Devron up and sucked them and the fly-things through, with Angela and Madison close behind. Larn and Jasper raced through the gap, and The Gate shuddered and closed.

Tim landed heavily, his breath whooshing out as he hit the ground. He fought for air, gasping and choking until his chest eased and he could breathe properly. He felt a sudden, sharp pain in the back of his hand and he looked down to see the horrid fly-thing still there, clinging to him. He yelled and shook it off. It dropped to the ground and, like the red lizard had done, shrank as Tim stared in disgust.

Devron! Those fly-things had attacked him. Tim jumped up and looked around. The Gatekeeper was still on the ground, with the fly-things all over him. Tim ran towards him and halted in amazement as Devron clambered to his feet. A blue-green haze surrounded him, and the fly-things battered vainly against it like moths at a lighted window. One by one, the creatures shrank to the size of large dragonflies, just like the rest of their kind in this world. A swarm of the tiny bee-type insects flew by, and all the fly-things set off in pursuit.

The haze around Devron dispersed quickly. 'Timoth,' he called. 'Are you all right? Why did you move away? Are the girls safe?'

Tim glanced down at the tiny lump on his hand. It itched a bit but it looked no bigger than a gnat bite. He tucked his hand into the pocket of his jeans. 'I'm okay,' he said, wondering why he wasn't telling Devron about the sting. 'They went for you, not me. I panicked. I didn't mean to move away from you. You used a mist-shield, didn't you? Like when you rescued Hamett from the fire at your cottage? Did they sting you?'

Devron shook his head. 'The shield worked. I'm fine. Look, Anaga and Madria are over there, with Jasper and Larn. Are you sure those things didn't touch you?'

Tim didn't answer Devron's question. Instead, he said, 'The Gate's gone again.'

Chapter 25

A Change in Behaviour

Devron sat down. Larn padded over to him and stood with his large head resting on the Gatekeeper's shoulder.

There was something about Devron's attitude that worried Tim. 'Are you sure the fly-things didn't hurt you?' he asked. 'There were an awful lot of them. It was just like in my dreams.'

'They didn't get through the mist-shield,' Devron assured him. 'I wasn't sure it would work but, fortunately, it appears they didn't like the dampness of the barrier.' He frowned. 'It didn't last as long as it should have done.'

'Did you see the way they shrank,' Madison said excitedly. 'Then they just flew off.'

Tim sat near Devron, and the girls and Jasper joined him. 'You saw them?'

Angela nodded. 'We heard them in Challenrah, by The Gate, but we both saw them once we were through here. No wonder you didn't like them. They were huge – and all those dangly legs…'

'Well, they're not huge any longer,' Madison said. 'And they've gone after the little bees. We're safe, aren't we, Devron?'

The Gatekeeper tugged gently at Larn's tufted ears and the leodan rumbled in pleasure. 'From those creatures, yes. If they didn't bother you last time you were here, I doubt they'll change that behaviour. Coming through The Gate into Challenrah caused the problem.'

'Speaking of Gates,' Tim said, 'why are you worrying about this one?'

'Because I can't sense it anywhere at all,' Devron confessed. 'I can "feel" every Gate on Challenrah. Even if I'm too far away to control it, I know when a Gateway forms and a Gate settles. I can't sense this one.' He turned to Angela. 'How about you, Anaga?'

Angela shook her head. 'I don't know where it is, Devron, but I couldn't find it last time. It was the hill I found, and then Madria drew The Gate.'

'How can it just vanish like that?' Madison asked. 'It disappears here but stays visible in Challenrah. How come?'

'There is a Gateway between one side of a Gate and the other,' Devron explained patiently. 'It's rather like a long cylinder or tube.'

'Like a wormhole?' Tim suggested, scratching inconspicuously at his hand.

Devron looked puzzled. 'A what?'

'A wormhole,' Tim repeated. 'Like in Star Trek, when... Never mind. Forget I said anything.'

'Go on, Devron,' Madison begged.

'A traveller passing through won't notice or feel the distance,' Devron continued, 'and the Gateway – the cylinder – is usually rigid and stays securely in place for as long as The Gate remains. However, on rare occasions the Gateway that forms is flexible. When that occurs, it's possible for one side to remain fixed while the other moves.'

'Oh, I see,' Madison said. 'One end of the tube goes somewhere else while the other stays where it was.'

'Precisely. It's very seldom that it happens at all, and one side doesn't usually disappear. Normally, it just moves slightly to a nearby location. Now, Nashena told me about the shifting geography of this place so, since we're on the hill, we'll wait here while you, Madria, work your magic again.'

Madison slipped her backpack off and opened it to take out her sketch pad. As he watched her, Tim's hand tingled and a warm, trickly feeling spread into his wrist. Hiding his actions from the others, he sneaked a look at his hand. The mark was no bigger than before, and there was no sign of any nasty blisters, but a streak of redness stretched from the back of his hand into his wrist. Tim prodded it gently and was relieved to find there was no pain. He looked up again just as Madison lifted out her pencil.

The ground trembled, startling all of them. Jasper whined and Larn yowled, and the two animals took off down the hill. The ground started to shake, moderately at first, and then so violently that Devron and the children were tumbled down the hill, coming to rest in an untidy heap when the shaking finally ceased.

Devron was first to his feet. 'Anyone hurt?' he asked as he checked the girls and Tim, and helped them up.

'Just a few bruises,' Angela said.

'Me too,' said Madison, rubbing her leg.

Devron turned to Tim. 'Timoth?'

'I'm fine,' Tim replied, pushing an anxious Jasper away while he brushed grass and soil from his clothing.

'This place is certainly full of surprises,' Devron commented, looking at where the hill had been moments ago.

As far as the eye could see, the land all around them stretched out in a huge, rolling plain. Close by, a wide stream twinkled in the sunlight.

'That stream's familiar but I can't see many bushes,' Angela said. 'That's good.'

'And I've got my backpack but I can't see my sketch pad and pencil,' Madison said, 'and that's *not* good.'

Devron turned to Angela. 'Anaga, can you "find" them?'

Angela stood with her eyes closed for a full minute. 'No. Sorry. My Gift is really unreliable here. Sometimes it works and sometimes it doesn't.'

'Not your fault,' Devron said. 'I couldn't hold the mist-shield for long and I can't find The Gate. Something about this land must be blocking powers like ours, at least for the time being. We'll have to do this the hard way. Come on.'

Keeping well within sight of each other, they started searching through the waist-high grass. Something crunched beneath Tim's foot and he crouched down warily in case it was some type of creature. It was Madison's pencil, broken into several pieces. He picked up the pointed section, turned ready to shout that he'd found it – and stuffed it into his pocket instead. He scuffed soil over the rest and walked on. A little farther off was the sketch pad, half-buried under a small rock. Tim ambled over and covered it up with more rocks. He pretended to carry on the search.

'Enough,' Devron called. 'Let's see if that water is fit to drink. We'll have a short rest, then look again. The pad and pencil must be around here somewhere.'

Tim sat with Jasper on the bank of the gently-flowing stream, a little way apart from the others. He could hear snatches of their conversation as Angela and Madison told Devron more about their previous visit here. Larn ambled over, sniffed at Tim and ran back to Devron.

'Don't sit with us then,' Tim muttered. 'We don't care, do we Jasper?'

The dog waved his tail and lay down, watching the rippling water. Tim pushed back the sleeve of his jacket and studied the progress of the redness up his arm. It had almost reached his elbow. The sun was hot but taking off his jacket would expose the inflammation. He rolled down his sleeve. His hand didn't hurt, nor did his arm. The redness would probably go away soon, he decided.

A slight breeze ruffled his hair and brought with it a strange but pleasant perfume. Tim reached out and tapped a purple, globular flower. It bobbed from side to side and gave off a sweet odour, rather like chocolate. Tim smiled. This place wasn't so bad after all. The countryside was beautiful, and the way it could alter from hill to plain and from grassland to forest was fascinating. Why had he been so scared to come back here? If you understood the land then it wouldn't harm you. The longer he stayed, the more he would learn about the flora and fauna. There must be a way to tame the bush-things and the red lizards, and he'd already started to communicate with a twiggy-person-creature. Challenrah seemed a distant memory, and his own world a mere dream. This land was where he belonged.

He didn't move when Angela called him to join them. Devron came to sit with him but Larn stayed by the girls.

'We'll find a way home,' the Gatekeeper said. 'Once Anaga or I can sense the hill, or even The Gate itself, we'll soon be out of here.'

'Were you reading my thoughts?' Tim asked sharply.

Devron frowned at the question. 'No. Of course not. Why?'

'Just don't,' Tim said.

Devron raised an eyebrow at Tim's tone but didn't reprimand him. 'Come,' he said. 'Sit and talk with us.'

Tim shook his head. 'Maybe later. I'd rather be on my own right now.'

Devron stood up. 'As you wish.' He bent to pat Tim on the shoulder but Tim leaned away. Devron stood looking down at him for a moment before going back to the girls.

Tim rolled onto his stomach, slithered forward down the bank and dangled his hands in the stream. On his last, hasty venture into the stream – when he'd fled from the bush-thing – the water had been shockingly cold but now he found it agreeably cool and soothing. A piece of water-weed glided up from the stream bed and weaved its way around his fingers. It tickled. Tim laughed. The others glanced across at him and he controlled his urge to go on giggling. The water-weed floated away downstream.

He shoved himself back from the water's edge and sat up. 'I hope The Gate never comes back,' he whispered to Jasper. 'I hope we can stay here forever.'

He watched, entranced, as a mass of dainty flowers pushed up through the grass near him on the stream's bank, their heart-shaped petals striped blue, pink and yellow. A swarm of bee-things flitted onto the flowers. Moments later, two fly-things descended to feast on the tiny bees. One fly-thing settled on Tim's hand, near to the site of the sting. He studied its gauzy wings, delicate legs and oval body. Its colouring was beautiful: shades of pink and purple, with a hint of shiny green. Only when Angela ran up to him did he shake it off.

'Was that a fly-thing?' she asked. 'Did it sting you?'

Tim shook his head. 'They don't sting in this world.'

Angela knelt by him. 'How do you know? They're smaller, but they might still sting. Wasps are small.'

Tim shrugged. 'It didn't sting,' he said, and added a lie. 'It only brushed across my hand.'

'As long as you're all right...'

'I'm fine,' Tim snapped. 'Why does everyone keep asking if I'm all right?'

Angela stood up. 'I came to tell you I think the hill's back, and Devron says he can feel The Gate even though we don't know where it is yet. Come on, Tim. We're going to try to get back to Challenrah.'

Tim's heart lurched. He didn't want to go back. He *couldn't* go back. He was part of this land. He had to stay.

'If Madison can't draw The Gate,' he said, trying to sound as if he cared, 'it won't materialise.' His hand went to his pocket where he'd tucked away the sharpened stub of the pencil. There was something underneath it – probably a candy wrapper he'd left in there.

'It might, with Devron there,' Angela said. 'Come on!' She dashed back to Devron and Madison.

Tim rose slowly. What if The Gate *did* appear? He couldn't just run away and hide; Devron would find him. The Gatekeeper would never leave him behind. Tim began to feel desperate. He had to think of a way to stop them from returning to Challenrah.

Chapter 26

Larn

Tim lagged behind as the group traipsed up the hill. When Devron turned to check on him, he slipped off his trainer and shook it, pretending there was a stone in it. He tried to hide his churning thoughts but the fluffy cloud he could create so easily in Challenrah refused to form. Devron couldn't sense The Gate properly; Tim hoped the Gatekeeper's telepathic powers weren't working either.

Almost at the summit of the hill, Tim heard a rustling sound and glanced back. A low, spreading bush behind him rose up and re-shaped into a huge sphere. Balancing on its four hind legs, it drummed its stubby front feet on the ground and charged. Tim knew he should be scared but all he felt was excitement as it thundered past, ignoring him and heading for Devron and the girls.

Devron spun round and stepped in front of Angela and Madison. The bush-creature was almost upon him when Larn leaped at it, knocking it off its feet and sending it hurtling down the steep slope like blown tumbleweed. The leodan followed, snapping at the leafy fur. Tim grabbed hold of Jasper's collar to prevent him joining in the chase.

At the foot of the hill, the bush-thing righted itself and turned to face Larn. A long, thick tongue shot out and slapped the leodan across the side of his face. Larn howled in pain but continued his attack on the bush. It gave up and fled, shedding bits of greeny-brown fur as it loped away. Larn took a few, unsteady steps after it, then swung round and plodded back up the hill. He passed Tim with barely a glance and made his way straight to Devron. As the Gatekeeper ran to meet him, the big cat collapsed and lay breathing noisily, his sides heaving.

Devron knelt by the animal, running his hands over the dense fur to find the wound. He touched Larn's face and his hands came away sticky with blood. Angela rummaged in her pocket and took out a tissue to pass to Devron. He pressed it gently over the leodan's injury. Larn whimpered faintly. Devron looked up and Tim was startled to see tears in the Gatekeeper's eyes.

'I can't help him,' Devron said in a strained voice. 'There's venom in that wound. My powers aren't strong enough here. I can't heal him. We have to get him home before it's too late for me to save him. We need The Gate.'

'Do something, Tim,' Angela begged. 'Help Devron.'

'If *his* talents won't work here, *mine* certainly won't,' Tim said.

'You could try,' Angela countered. 'What's wrong with you? Larn's your friend!'

She pulled another tissue from her pocket and Devron used it to wipe his hands. He stroked Larn's great head and then turned to Tim. 'Come here, Timoth,' he commanded.

Reluctantly, Tim obeyed. He expected Devron to tell him to try to help Larn, but the Gatekeeper stood up and caught hold of Tim's arm. 'What's that mark?' he asked.

Tim stood stiffly, resisting the desire to pull away. 'What mark?'

'The one on your neck.' Devron ran his finger down the side of Tim's neck. The touch didn't hurt but Tim flinched. 'Take off your jacket, Timoth.'

The Gatekeeper's talents might have been weak in this land but his air of authority wasn't. Tim obeyed. Angela and Madison gasped in horror at the livid, red streak that ran from Tim's right hand all the way up his arm. Across his shoulder it was hidden by his tee-shirt but it was clearly visible again up the side of his neck.

'What did that?' Madison asked.

Devron's orange gaze seemed to bore right into Tim. He took a step away from the Gatekeeper and answered, 'A fly-thing.'

It was a long time since Tim had seen Devron look so severe. 'You told me they hadn't touched you. When were you stung? Was it as we came through The Gate?'

Tim nodded sulkily and scuffed the toe of his trainer into the grass. Why were they all glaring at him? They were the intruders in this world, not him. All he wanted was to walk off and live his life here without interference. 'It doesn't hurt,' he said defensively. 'Leave me alone.'

Devron's gaze softened. 'It's infected you, Timoth,' he said. 'Those creatures changed when they entered Challenrah, as did the *raffakins* in your world, and that sting has changed you in this land.' He paused and bent to stroke Larn again before saying, 'I can't heal you here, Timoth. You'll have to fight its effects yourself. Don't let it win.'

Tim's brow furrowed. What was he talking about? Infection? Fighting? It was hard to sort out his muddled thoughts.

Jasper whined and went to lie tucked against the stricken leodan. Tim looked down at the suffering animal. The big cat's breath rasped in his throat and his huge paws twitched restlessly. A twinge of sympathy woke inside Tim. Larn had befriended him from the first time they'd met. It was wrong to see him like this. Tim wanted to make sure everyone stayed in this land… but he'd have to watch the poor animal die… or he could try to help… Somewhere deep inside him he grieved for Larn but the feeling that he must stay here at all costs was almost overwhelming.

'Don't just stand there, Tim!' Angela cried. 'Do something!'

Devron drew her to him and put his arm around her shoulders. 'It's not his fault, Anaga. The fly-creature's poison is in his system and he can't control his actions or thoughts.'

Couldn't control his actions or thoughts? Tim didn't like the sound of that. What had happened to free will? He wanted to be able to make his own decisions. Had that fly-thing really affected his reasoning?

'Remember the old Gate, Timoth,' Devron said. 'Think about how hard it was for you to choose to help me. You were strong enough to make the right decision then, and you're strong enough to fight this poison inside you.'

Tim almost turned to walk away but Devron's words were strangely compelling. Choosing to side with Devron and help close the sabotaged Gate had been the most difficult decision he'd ever made. He'd known the old Gate would disappear once it was double-locked, and he'd thought at the time he'd be shut out of Challenrah forever. He'd done it, though. He'd helped to save Challenrah from the *raffakins*. It was different now: he couldn't help Larn even if he chose to try. Why should he bother?

He stuffed his reddened hand into his pocket and the point of the pencil jabbed his finger. Madison's pencil. If he gave it to her, she still wouldn't be able to draw Vallend's Gate – her sketch pad was hidden somewhere under a little pile of rocks. A faint, unwanted pang of guilt surfaced briefly. He pushed it away. He would give her the stub of pencil; at least it would look then as if he was making an effort to help.

Pulling it out of his pocket was surprisingly hard; not because it was stuck there but because Tim's muscles didn't want to cooperate. Anything remotely to do with bringing back The Gate was abhorrent to him. His fingers trembled as he finally extricated the bit of pencil and held it out.

'Forgot I'd found this,' he lied.

Madison walked over, took the pencil out of his hand and shot away as if he was radioactive. 'Where's my sketch pad?' she asked.

'How should I know?' Tim retorted. All three of them stared at him and he said, 'I think I saw it a minute ago, on my way up here. It was near some rocks.'

Why was he giving them even this much information? If they found the pad she'd draw The Gate and they'd make him go back with them. He pointed down the slope. 'Over there.'

He led the way to where he knew he'd buried the sketch pad but the little mound of stones had gone, torn away in the changing landscape, and there was no sign of the pad. Tim breathed a sigh of relief as the rest of the group trudged disconsolately back to Larn and Jasper. Tim followed slowly.

Devron sat down by Larn and took the animal's head onto his lap. 'Timoth,' he said softly, 'I know it must be hard for you, but if there is anything you *can* do then now's the time. Larn is slipping away from me.'

Tim shoved his hand back into his pocket and fingered the candy wrapper. Could Madison draw on that or would the paper be too shiny? Should he take the chance? It would be best to look at the paper and then decide what to do with it. He turned his back on the group and forced his fingers to close on the paper. It seemed to take forever to pull it out a millimetre at a time.

He stared in amazement at the scrap of paper in his hand. It wasn't a wrapper but part of the drawing Madison had done when she'd been grounded – the picture of Vallend's Gate, partly-open, where Tim had been the only one to see mist and dark shapes in the gap. Why had he seen that? Had it been a warning about the dangers of this land? The drawing was faded and the paper crumpled and torn. It must have been left in his pocket when his mum had washed his jeans. It was amazing it had survived at all.

An image of his mother came into his mind: his mother with Cassie. Cassie was laughing and calling out silly words, only half-understandable. She couldn't quite manage Tim's name yet, and in his mind he heard her calling out: 'Immy! Immy play!' He remembered how poorly she'd been and how desperately he'd wanted to heal her. He had helped then, if only by loving his little sister. No, it had been more than that. His healing talent *had* made a difference; he was sure of that. Could he make a difference now?

He turned slowly to face the group. No one was watching him; they were all kneeling by Larn. The great cat was very still.

'Is he...?' Tim began. He brushed away an unexpected tear.

Devron spoke without looking up. 'He's alive, but he's fading fast. Come and say farewell to him, Timoth.'

Tim didn't want Larn to die, but he didn't want to leave this beautiful and fascinating land. The amazing creatures here weren't so deadly after all – or were they? The bush-thing had by-passed him but it had been intent on harming the others. Its tongue had wounded Larn and the venom was killing him. Tim was certain now that the mist and dark shapes he'd seen in Madison's picture had indeed been a warning. Why had he never thought of that before?

He was holding the last remnant of that drawing and it could give the group their only chance of bringing back The Gate. If Devron could get Larn back into Challenrah, he might be able to save him.

Tim had a choice to make, but it wasn't going to be easy.

Chapter 27

Escape

Tim found tears running down his cheeks. He didn't know whether they were for Larn or for the thought of leaving this land. He took a step towards Devron and the others, and his hand, arm and neck hurt viciously. He moved back, and the pain went away. He tried again, and this time the pain was unbearable. He staggered back, and the hurt eased immediately. He had made up his mind to hand over the paper but he couldn't take it to Madison because the pain was too great when he moved forwards.

He tried to call her name, but his hand suddenly felt as if it was on fire and his arm and neck flared with agony. Struggling to be brave, he attempted to call Angela and then Devron, but the awful pain stopped him. He took another step back and stayed silent. The pain went away. He realised with growing horror that Devron was right: the fly-thing's sting had put into his body some substance that was indeed affecting him. Not only was it changing his behaviour, it was also linking him to this world, and he suspected that the longer he stayed the stronger the connection would become. The land he'd thought was so wonderful was not going to release him willingly – and that wasn't fair. He wanted to make up his own mind about whether or not to stay here.

Jasper left Larn's side, trotted over to Tim and licked his good hand. 'What do I do now, Jasper?' Tim whispered.

His arm and neck hurt a bit when he spoke to the dog, but not as much as when he tried to step forwards or call to the others. Why weren't they looking his way? Didn't they know he was in trouble? He rubbed at his neck. It would be so easy to give in and accept that he should remain here, but that would mean the others would have to stay too. The creatures of this world no longer posed any threat to him but he was sure the bush-thing, the red lizard, and probably the twiggy-person-creature, would be deadly to the others. Could he really allow Devron, Angela and Madison to be trapped and in danger here forever? Devron was vital to Challenrah, wasn't he? What would happen if he didn't return there? How would they manage without him?

Despite finally accepting that he was being influenced by the fly-thing's poison, Tim still found it hard to ignore the appeal of the land. If he stayed, the pain would go away and he could be happy in this world, but Larn was sick because he'd defended them all from the bush-thing and Tim didn't want Larn to die. Maybe Challenrah wasn't so bad. All their Gifts worked there and Devron could save Larn and take away the pain in

Tim's hand and arm and neck. Here, the only reliable power was Madison's talent for bringing her drawings to life.

Jasper's long ears drooped sadly. He sat and gazed up at Tim, and Tim had an idea that just might work. He and Angela had taught Jasper to carry a toy from one of them to the other – in exchange for a treat – and the young dog loved that game. 'Here, Jasper,' he whispered. It took a great effort of will to hold out the crumpled paper. 'Take it to Angela.'

Jasper sniffed the paper suspiciously. It wasn't one of the toys he was used to.

'Take it,' Tim urged softly. If the dog didn't oblige soon, Tim knew he'd change his mind and hide the drawing from the others. 'Take it to Angela,' he whispered. His hand began to tremble with the strain of holding out the crumpled sketch of The Gate.

Jasper seized hold of the paper and trotted off to Angela. She took it from his mouth and Tim could see the sudden hope in her expression.

'Maddie,' she shouted, although Madison was standing right next to her. 'Look! The Gate! Your picture of The Gate. Quick! Fill in the missing bits.'

Madison didn't question where Tim had found the paper or why he'd chosen to hand it over. She plonked her backpack on the ground to rest on and scribbled frantically. Despite her haste and the creases in the paper, the picture took shape rapidly.

A faint humming sounded close to Tim and a swarm of fly-things buzzed around his head and shoulders, their dangly legs tickling his face. Devron was occupied with Larn, and Angela was intent on watching Madison. Tim couldn't call out to alert them but it seemed the fly-things

218

were only interested in him. He sensed no danger from them. Their dance was mesmerising and Tim felt the pull of the land once again. He resisted strongly. It had to be *his* choice to remain here or to leave, and for Angela, Madison and Devron – and especially for Larn – he had chosen to leave.

'Go away,' he murmured. He had to speak quietly to stop the pain coming back but he wasn't about to yield to their enchantment. They persisted in hovering around him and he grew angry. 'Get lost!' he said. 'Fly off. Find someone else to annoy!'

As if obeying his wish, the swarm circled him once more and then zoomed off, hunting a flight of tiny bee-insects that had appeared on the hillside.

The Gate became visible close to them. Transparent at first, it solidified as Madison shaded it in on her drawing. Through the slightly-open Gate, a shaft of Challendrian sunlight shone directly onto Devron. He looked up and drew in a deep breath. 'Go,' he ordered. 'I'll bring Larn.'

Madison snatched up her belongings and dashed for the opening. Angela hesitated. 'You can't,' she said. 'He's too heavy.'

'Our sunlight's helped us both,' Devron told her. 'If he can get to his feet, I'll be able to guide him. Go, child!' Angela ran after Madison, and Devron turned his attention to Tim. 'You too, Timoth. You can't stay here. It's not safe. That poison in your system will kill you. You have to come with us.'

Without understanding how he knew, Tim realised The Gatekeeper was right. The poison that had made this land seem so wonderful might actually kill him if he stayed here too long. He'd been only too ready to escape from this land after their first visit. Why was he so reluctant to leave now? It could only be due to the fly-thing's poison. That wasn't going to stop him, though. He'd made his choice and he was sticking to it.

He took one step towards The Gate – and fell to his knees in pain. He crawled on for the length of a couple of paces and stopped. He couldn't go any farther. It was too hard.

A bearded figure loomed over him, dragged him upright and slung him over a strong shoulder. Dangling like a sack of potatoes, he was lugged through The Gate and deposited on the red-tinted grass beyond. Jasper barked and danced around him. He squirmed into a sitting position in time to see the figure – Vallend – sprint back to help Devron carry Larn out of the land beyond The Gate. A violet cloud surrounded the two men and the leodan, showing Tim that they were using some sort of power to help with the weight of the big cat.

The Gatekeepers barely had time to set down their furry burden when The Gate launched itself into the air. Trailing the low fence like decorative strings on a kite, it twisted round and round, raining down shards of wood. Tim groaned as he lifted his arms to shield himself and Jasper. Everyone else crouched low and covered their heads until the onslaught was over.

Shattered pieces of The Gate and fence lay strewn on the ground. They glowed a sickly green, then turned to dust and vanished completely. The dreadful pain in Tim's arm and neck diminished to a mild discomfort. 'Everyone all right?' he heard Vallend call out.

Jasper licked Tim's face and he pushed the dog away gently. A strange noise was coming from near where The Gate had stood and Tim looked across to see Parrin and Syeesha prowling in circles around Devron and their injured cub. The two leodans were mewling softly and Tim's stomach turned somersaults. He'd delayed the return to Challenrah. He was to blame if Larn was dead. Finding movement hard, not because of any pain but because he was scared of what he'd find, he stumbled over to where Devron sat cradling Larn's great head.

The Gatekeeper glanced up at Tim's approach. 'Timoth?' he said. 'Are you well?'

Tim nodded. He didn't care about himself. He just wanted Larn to be all right.

'Sit,' said Devron. His tone made it a request rather than an order.

Tim hesitated. After his behaviour in that other land, what right had he to be counted as part of the group again? He fought to form his question. 'Larn? Are we too late? Can Vallend–'

'Vallend's busy checking the area with the Wardens. Come and sit with me. Your help will speed things along.'

Speed things along? Larn could be healed? Tim almost tripped over in his haste to obey the Gatekeeper.

Close to, Tim could see the mark across Larn's face. The wound was no longer bleeding and the torn flesh showing beneath the thick fur was already knitting cleanly. Tim placed his hands next to Devron's on the big cat's head. He could feel only a faint residue of the toxin that had so nearly taken the animal's life. His hands grew warm as he concentrated on removing those last traces of venom.

Larn stirred and purred loudly. A smile lit Devron's face. 'He'll be fine now. Good work, Timoth.'

Parrin and Syeesha stopped their plaintive crying and crowded in to lick their offspring. Larn stood up, dislodging Devron and Tim, and tottered off shakily to lie with his parents.

Tim shuffled away from Devron and sat with his arms around his drawn-up knees. He buried his head in his arms to hide his sobs of relief. Devron rose slowly and walked towards Vallend and the others, pausing briefly to run a hand gently over Tim's head. The residual ache faded from his hand, arm and neck.

Chapter 28

Justice and a Feast

Tim stood behind the waist-high metal bar on the raised platform of the large hall in the courthouse, trying not to show how scared he was as the red-robed High Justice took her seat on the ornate chair at the centre of the stage. As before, the room held no audience but for a few guards in their black-braided, blue tunics. Tim grasped the bar and held on firmly to stop himself shaking. At least Devron was here this time

The voice of the High Justice carried clearly throughout the hall. 'Timoth, apprentice to Gatekeeper Devron, I have heard the testimony of our Gatekeeper and have learned of your part in ridding Challenrah of the invading creatures that threatened our crops and our people. It has also been brought to my attention that you did not first enter that new land of your own volition but were drawn through by a mighty wind. Is it your sworn word that this is the truth?'

Tim gripped the bar even more tightly and cleared his throat. 'Yes,' he said as loudly as he could manage. 'Yes, it is.'

'You did, however, go back there…'

Tim panicked at her tone and looked up at Devron. The Gatekeeper placed a reassuring hand on his shoulder. Tim turned his attention back to what the High Justice was saying.

'…and this time of your own choice, in order to aid our cause. Your courage, and that of your friends, is commended. In light of your actions, and on the recommendation of Gatekeeper Devron and his Wardens, the sentence of banishment from Challenrah is hereby rescinded.'

'Rescinded?' Tim echoed softly. 'What does that mean?'

'Withdrawn,' Devron said.

Weak with relief, Tim sagged against the metal bar.

The High Justice continued, 'Henceforth, and for as long as you obey our laws, you may enter our land if and when a Gate will allow you to do so. You are dismissed from this court.' She stood up and, with a swish of robes, stalked off the platform.

Tim turned and flung his arms around Devron, then pushed himself away, embarrassed. 'Sorry.'

Devron smiled. 'Come. The others are waiting for us with the temarals.'

'Are we leaving straight away?' Tim asked.

Devron nodded. 'I've done all I need to here, for the present anyway. I think we'll all rest better when we're home. More questions can wait until later, Timoth.' He led the way from the courthouse.

Tim's eyes widened in surprise when he saw Vallend standing outside waiting for them.

'I'll leave you two to talk,' Devron said. 'Don't be long, Timoth. Meet me at the end of the street in a few minutes.' He walked off, leaving Tim with Vallend.

Vallend broke the uncomfortable silence. 'So, you're allowed back? Justified, I think, after your actions concerning the flying creatures.'

Tim met the Gatekeeper's gaze. 'Thanks,' he said. *Why didn't you admit you'd let them through The Gate?* he wanted to ask. Instead, he said, 'Thanks for coming through The Gate and getting me out.'

'It was a very strange land,' Vallend said. 'It called to me even in those moments I was there.'

'Called to you?'

'That doesn't matter now,' Vallend went on. 'I just came to check on High Justice Rellia's verdict and to bid you farewell.'

'Oh. Right. Thanks,' Tim said. 'Aren't you coming back with the rest of us?'

Vallend shook his head. 'This is my home village. I'm staying here for a while.' He rubbed a hand across his beard.

Tim stared at an angry red mark on the Gatekeeper's wrist. 'Were you stung?' he blurted out.

Vallend frowned. 'Stung? No. Why?'

'Your wrist,' Tim said. 'That mark.'

Vallend looked at his arm. 'Oh, that. A splinter from The Gate when it shattered.'

'But why hasn't it healed? Can I help?'

'Devron has already offered,' Vallend said. 'I told him to leave it. Gatekeepers usually heal quickly from minor injuries.'

'But...'

'No, Timoth. It'll heal in time. Meanwhile, it reminds me what can happen if I fail in my responsibilities. Right now, I need that reminder.'

Tim pointed to the tiny, fading mark on the back of his own hand. 'Me too. I nearly let everyone down.'

'Nearly, from what I've heard,' said Vallend, 'but it's making the right choice in the end that counts. We should both remember that.' He reached to shake Tim's hand. 'A human gesture of goodwill, I'm told.'

Tim nodded and shook the proffered hand. Vallend turned and strode away. For a moment Tim stood where he was, then he ran to join Devron.

The familiar setting of Devron's cottage was comforting. As he walked down the short path to the front door, Tim let out a deep, satisfied sigh and shrugged his shoulders to relax muscles that had been tense for ages.

'Go and wash,' Kallyn instructed the children. 'Nashena's home; she'll show you the way. Devron – go and rest while Jeznia, Carradin and I sort out something for us to eat.'

Tim trotted upstairs after Angela and Madison, smiling at the way Devron – in command in every other way – meekly obeyed Kallyn.

Madison turned to Angela. 'Does Nashena live here?' she asked softly when Nashena had left them at the top of the stairs.

'Yes. Hamett too.'

'But they're Devron and Kallyn's niece and nephew, aren't they?'

Angela gave her a gentle push towards the wash-room. 'Yes. Their parents died when Nashena was a baby. Their mum was Kallyn's older sister.'

'What happened?' Madison asked.

'I don't know. An accident of some sort. Hurry up, Madria. I'm hungry.'

With most of the dust from the ride washed from their hands and faces, Tim and the girls hurried downstairs to join the adults. Tim halted so suddenly in the doorway of the back room that Angela bumped into him. She and Madison shoved past him to see what he was looking at. A long table was set with trays of food and jugs of drinks.

'I thought there was a food shortage here,' Tim said.

'There is,' Kallyn responded, 'but less so in the village we've just left. The High Justice arranged for food packs to be given to us before we set off.'

Tim's mouth dropped open. 'The High Justice? But she's so...'

'Stern, I think is the word you're searching for,' said Devron from behind Tim.

Tim turned to the Gatekeeper. 'Er... yes. Stern.'

Devron's orange eyes twinkled with amusement. 'She is indeed – when she needs to be.' He became serious again. 'High Justice Rellia and I have known each other for many years, Timoth. She's willing to listen to all sides of a story and she's fair in her judgements.'

From inside the room, Carradin called out, 'The pair of you work well together, governing this place, Gatekeeper. Now, come and eat before I tuck in and leave nothing for you.'

Tim's mouth watered as Kallyn organised places for everyone. She and Carradin handed round filled plates. Fragrant steam rose from a small pie in the centre of Tim's plate and he decided to taste that first, almost burning his tongue in his haste to try it. The pastry was delicious and whatever vegetables made up the filling left a delightful, tangy taste in his mouth. Carradin grinned at Tim's expression and handed him another of the pies. Tim ate half and was about to be noble enough to give some to Jasper when he noticed that Kallyn had just set down a bowl of food and some water for the hungry young dog. Tim ate the rest of his pie as he watched Jasper wolfing down the food.

Carradin settled himself next to Devron. 'You said you were on the other side of The Gate for a couple of hours?'

Devron finished a mouthful of cheese before replying. 'Yes, at least that.'

'Minutes only on this side,' Carradin said.

'So Vallend told me,' returned Devron. 'And I think that made all the difference to your being able to control The Gate until we were back.'

'It wasn't easy, even for that short time,' Kallyn stated. 'Vallend did a good job coordinating the effort.'

Devron chuckled. 'High praise, coming from you.' Kallyn pulled a face at him. He laughed, and then continued in a more serious tone, 'We would have been in real trouble without his help at The Gate. Timoth could barely move, and I couldn't lift Larn until Vallend joined his power with what little I had in that land. It's fortunate we were so close to the opening that he didn't lose his Gifts and that mine returned as soon as we crossed the threshold.'

Carradin stood up and poured some juice into glasses. The tantalising aroma of spiced fruit wafted across the room. 'We've seen some strange happenings over the years we've been with you, Gatekeeper,' the Warden commented, handing round the drinks, 'but I never thought to see a Gate behave like that one.'

'Has it gone for good?' Jeznia asked, speaking for the first time since they'd sat down to eat.

'It has,' confirmed Devron. 'There's no trace of the Gateway left behind.'

'Good,' said Tim, and pretended to be occupied with eating when they all looked at him.

'Good indeed,' agreed Carradin, and Tim smiled.

Jeznia asked the question that was on Tim's mind. 'What will happen to Vallend?'

Devron put down his plate and leaned back in his chair. 'His crime was not reporting the entry of those creatures. He couldn't see them properly but he *did* know *something* had passed through The Gate when it first opened and he suspected that whatever had invaded was around Timoth's Gate on a couple of occasions. The crops began to fail soon after Vallend's Gate appeared but no one saw any connection between that and his Gate.'

'I bet the fly-things got bigger and nastier the longer they stayed here,' Tim said. 'And maybe Vallend's Gate started trying to force its way open recently because it wanted to let more of them through into Challenrah.'

'I saw how shocked Vallend was when he learned how dangerous they were,' Jeznia said, 'but even if they'd been the most harmless creatures imaginable, he should have informed you straight away, Devron.'

'Too arrogant,' Carradin commented. 'Too sure he could handle the situation.'

'Since he couldn't see them properly, he tried to convince himself that nothing was there after all,' Devron said. 'As it stands, his actions at The Gate this morning have mitigated the offence...' He saw Tim's puzzled expression and paused to explain. 'Mitigated means moderated or lessened. Anyway, I'll no longer have him as my Second. If he's to be allowed to remain a Gatekeeper, he'll have to agree to re-train and re-take his vows.'

'He's a proud man,' Carradin observed. 'Will he do that?'

'He will if he wants to be a Gatekeeper badly enough,' Devron answered. 'I left him to think it over.'

'I think he'll do it,' Tim said. 'Will it mean more work for you, Devron? You'll have his Wardens to supervise as well as your own, won't you?'

'Devron's in overall charge anyway, Timoth,' Kallyn told him. 'But don't worry; we'll help him when we can.'

'What about the bees... I mean the brezzers?' Angela asked.

'The population will recover now the predators have gone,' Devron assured her. 'The Wardens will appoint attendants to prepare special hives and plants for them until their numbers are sufficient for them to manage without our help.'

'A bit like our bee garden project,' Madison commented.

Jeznia reached for a slice of yellow fruit that looked to Tim like melon but smelled like blackcurrant. The Warden saw him watching and passed him a slice to try. Her sleeve fell back as she did so.

230

'You've still got a faint scar,' Tim said.

Jeznia glanced down at the blister-shaped mark above her wrist. 'Yes, but nothing more than that, thanks to you and Devron.'

Tim grinned. 'Devron and I reckon the infection was finally easy to clear because the fly-things aren't in Challenrah anymore.'

'Well, I feel fine now, and to prove it I shall have some more glantral.' She took another slice of the juicy, yellow fruit.

Hunger satisfied at last, Tim and the three girls went out into the small back garden, with Jasper following. Larn leapt the back gate and bounded at Tim, knocking him to the ground.

'Oof! Get off Larn,' Tim spluttered. The big feline moved aside and Tim sat up and ruffled the leodan's fur. 'I'm so sorry, Larn,' he said quietly. 'I'm glad we're friends again.'

With Jasper lying next to Larn, and the girls chatting under the shade of the tree near the gate, Tim sat quietly, contemplating all that had happened.

'The sun will be down in about an hour,' Nashena called across to Tim. 'Are you going to stay? I know time moves on in your world after dark here, but Anaga told me you and Madria had arranged to stay at her home so your parents won't be worried. You could stop here overnight and have another whole day here before you have to return.'

A night in Challenrah? Sleep here and have more time before going home? The prospect was appealing. Perhaps Devron would have time to teach Tim more about using his Gifts. He looked at Angela and Madison, and they nodded enthusiastically.

He was about to agree to Nashena's suggestion when he felt a peculiar sensation running through him. Had that third pie he'd eaten upset his digestion? No – the feeling was in his chest and head, not his stomach. He stood up unsteadily just as Devron came hastening out of the cottage.

'You noticed that?' Devron queried.

Tim nodded. 'What is it?'

Instead of answering, the Gatekeeper instructed, 'Study the sensation, then see if you can tell me.'

Tim did as he was told. 'It's my Gate,' he said after a moment.

Devron nodded approval. 'Good. You're learning quickly.'

'But what's wrong with it?'

'Nothing's wrong, Timoth,' said Devron. 'The Gate is just ready to go.'

Tim stared at him. 'Go? It can't go. The old Gate stayed for generations.'

'They usually choose their own time to form and to leave, Timoth,' Devron reminded him. 'And this one won't remain here much longer. I need to get you all back now.'

Chapter 29

Worlds Apart

Tim expected Devron to summon the temarals for a frantic ride to The Gate but Devron chose to walk there.

'The Gate will wait for you,' he assured them, 'and we'll be there well before dark. Walking rather than riding will give you a little extra time here.' He whistled for Parrin and Syeesha and the big cats appeared from somewhere in the long grass.

Tim looked up hopefully. 'Will The Gate wait if we stay with you overnight?'

The Gatekeeper shook his head. 'No.'

'But…'

'I, too, wish you could stay longer, Timoth,' he said. 'Perhaps someday that will be possible.'

With Kallyn, Nashena, Jeznia and Carradin all accompanying them, the walk to The Gate was over too quickly for Tim. He hung back with Jasper and Larn as Evrald and Hamett came to meet the Gatekeeper.

Something buzzed past Tim's ear and he spun round with a yelp before exhaling in relief.

'What is it?' Devron asked.

'Just a bee... er... a brezzer,' Tim said.

'We've seen two or three around in the last hour,' Hamett reported.

'That's good,' said Devron. 'Let's hope it's the start of their revival. Timoth, come to The Gate.'

Reluctantly, Tim started forwards – and fell over as Larn grabbed his leg. The leodan held on with a gentle but very firm grip. 'Let go, Larn,' Tim said. 'I don't want to leave but I have to.'

The leodan rumbled a protest but released Tim's leg. Tim scrambled up, trying in vain not to redden at the laughter from the rest of the group. He brushed grass off his jeans and went over to Devron. The Gate looked much as it had from the beginning, except for tiny golden sparkles throughout the wood.

Tim decided to practise his telepathy. *Is that because you're near it?* he asked Devron.

It's for both of us, came the reply. *Open it, Timoth.'*

Me? But I can't–

You have your badge? Devron queried.

Yes, of course.

Then fasten it on and open The Gate.

Could it be that easy? He just had to wear his Gatekeeper badge? He rummaged in his jacket pocket and brought out the golden, Gate-shaped badge. He'd never polished it but it was as shiny as the day Devron had given it to him. His fingers trembled a bit as he pinned it onto the left shoulder of his jacket.

'The Gate is ready, Timoth,' Devron said aloud. 'Open it.'

Torn between the desperate desire to stay and the excitement of learning how to open The Gate, Tim forced himself to touch the padlock as he had seen Vallend do, then he reached for the latch.

'A stabilised Gate like this one just needs a Gatekeeper's permission to open,' Devron explained. 'Give it your consent. You'll need to work swiftly. It won't wait much longer.'

'Do we both need to lock it at the same time?' Tim asked. 'Like we did with the old Gate?'

'No. This Gate poses no danger; it just wants to leave. Close the padlock on your side. The Gate will do the rest. Open it now, Timoth.'

Tim swallowed hard against the lump in his throat. *Open for us, please,* he thought to The Gate. *We have to go home before you vanish.*

Under his hand, the latch warmed and lifted, and The Gate swung open slowly and gently.

'Wow!' exclaimed Tim. 'It worked! Thanks, Gate.'

Angela and Madison hastily finished saying their goodbyes and slipped through the opening. Tim took a step forwards and then stopped. 'I don't want to go,' he said.

'Challenrah has that effect on visitors,' Devron said with a smile. 'At least, it does on visitors who are welcome here. Yet again, you have my gratitude for all your help. It seems each time you come to us you have hard choices to make. I'm thankful you've been strong enough to make the right decisions. Take pride in that. Go now, Timoth, and don't forget us.'

'Forget you?' Tim repeated. 'I could never do that. And I will be able to come back, won't I?'

The chain on the gatepost startled Tim by rattling loudly. It drowned out Devron's answer. Tim felt again the odd vibration that had run through him in Devron's garden. The chain rattled again. It had never moved by itself before and Tim guessed it was warning him that The Gate would close and disappear any second. He attached the leash to Jasper's collar and the young dog yanked him out of Challenrah. The Gate shut behind him with a soft thud that sounded like a sigh.

Angela and Madison were waiting for him on the deserted Strand. Tim closed the padlock, pocketed the key and stood gazing at The Gate. Although the golden sparkles had gone, the wood, chain and latch looked normal enough. The Gate hadn't vanished as he'd expected it to.

'Perhaps it's changed its mind,' he said.

Angela came a step nearer. 'What do you mean?'

'It's still here, isn't it? Maybe it wants to stay after all.' He took out his key and tried it in the padlock.

Madison peered over his shoulder. 'Are you opening it again?'

'I'm trying to,' Tim answered, 'but the key won't fit.' He straightened up and tucked the key away. 'I daren't force it in; that might bend the key, or it could get stuck in the padlock.'

'Well, at least we're all back in time to really stay at Angela's,' Madison said. 'And look – the Strand's getting busy. We'd better go. We can come back and try again tomorrow.'

'S'pose so,' Tim agreed grudgingly. The sound of voices drew his attention away from The Gate. Walkers and joggers, and a few cyclists, were heading in both directions along the Strand. He turned back in time to see the wooden slats and gateposts fade into transparency. The chain rattled once more, softly this time, and Tim felt a slight jolt in his chest as The Gate disappeared completely.

Tim, Angela and Madison sat together in Angela's back room. An eventful day had passed in Challenrah but here in their own world it was still early afternoon. Val had offered them a late lunch but after the feast at Devron's cottage the only one who was still hungry was Jasper.

Angela's mum and grandfather stayed with them during the rest of the afternoon, eager to hear all that had happened in Challenrah. Later, when the children's appetites returned, they all shared a light supper before David and Val left Tim and the girls to talk amongst themselves. They didn't talk, though. Now that the excitement of telling David and Val about their adventures had worn off, Tim was trying to come to terms with his Gate disappearing, and it looked to him as if Angela and Madison were as disconsolate as he was at the thought of being away from Challenrah and not knowing if they'd ever be able to return.

'Thank you,' Madison said at last.

Tim looked up. 'What for?'

'For taking me with you,' Madison replied.

Tim was about to say that he'd not had much choice in the matter, but he held back the words. Instead, he said, 'Thank you for getting us out of that land – twice. If you hadn't been with us, we'd have been stuck there.'

Madison's smile lit up her face. 'It was a great feeling when the drawings came to life. And the food that appeared on our first visit there…'

'Grey, but not bad,' Angela said with a laugh. 'Saved us from going hungry.'

Madison turned to Tim again. 'Thank you for giving me the paper and pencil, Tim. You said the paper had been washed in your pocket, didn't you? I'm amazed it hadn't disintegrated completely.'

Tim grinned at her. 'Your drawings are special, Maddie. David said so, and he's right. Your Gate picture was there when we needed it.'

Madison beamed at the praise. 'Still, it must have been hard for you to hand it over.'

'It was,' Tim admitted. 'I didn't want Vallend's Gate to come back. I know it was only the fly-thing's poison affecting me, but I wanted to stay there.' He shuffled back in his chair until his legs dangled just off the floor. 'I'm sorry. You could all have been stranded there because of me. And Larn could have died.'

'Well, we weren't and he didn't,' Angela said. 'You made the right choice in the end and that's what matters.'

Tim smiled. 'That's what Vallend and Devron said.'

Angela's mother popped her head round the door. 'Bedtime, everyone,' she said. 'Madison and Tim, have you texted your parents?'

'We've called them,' Madison said.

'Good. Madison, you're with Angela in her room. Tim, you're in the room next to Dad. Angela will show you. Oh, I nearly forgot; there's a letter here for you, Angela. The envelope has an official-looking logo. Were you expecting something during the holidays?'

'No,' Angela replied. 'I don't think so.'

'Wait there. I'll go and get it.' She hurried out of the room.

'That's odd,' Tim observed. 'When I called home, Peter said there was a letter there for me. He said Cassie'd tried to eat it!'

'I've got one as well,' Madison added. 'Caleb told me.'

Val appeared with the letter and handed it to Angela. 'Open it,' she urged. 'Your granddad and I have been longing to know what it's about.'

Angela slit open the envelope with her thumb and drew out the letter.

'What is it?' Tim asked. 'Are we in trouble?'

Madison nudged him in the ribs. 'Guilty conscience?'

'Shut up, you two,' Angela said. 'It's about the ecology competition.'

Tim and Madison crowded closer. 'What's it say?'

'We've won!' Angela said. She handed Tim the letter.

'"We are pleased to inform you that your project *Bee Happy* has been awarded first place in the City of Oceanside Council Junior Ecology Project",' Tim read out.

'We've won?' Madison queried. 'Really? You're not joking?'

Tim passed the letter to her. 'See for yourself. It's signed by the Mayor.'

Madison's yell of delight made them all laugh. 'They're giving the school the funding for a bee garden,' she said. 'And we get to design it. Amazing!'

'We wouldn't have won without your illustrations, Maddie,' Tim said. 'And the bee garden was your idea.'

'Yeah, but you and Angela did most of the research. Team effort, Timothy. Like in Challenrah. All three of us. Team effort.' She gave the letter back to Angela. 'Put that away somewhere safe so it doesn't disappear overnight! Better still, frame it and put it on the wall.'

'Whatever you're going to do with it can wait until tomorrow,' Angela's mother said. 'Go on, the three of you. Wash, and bed.' She ushered them out of the back room and up the stairs.

Tim dreamed he was back in Challenrah. The red-tinted grass was soft and springy beneath his bare feet. He was sitting on the hillside with Jasper on one side and Larn on the other. Brezzers buzzed busily on and off the numerous flowers dotted all over the slope. The orange sun was high overhead and contentment flooded through him. This was how Challenrah should look – fertile and beautiful.

Nearby, Devron and the Wardens sat chatting with Angela and Madison. Tim smiled. He didn't mind Madison being here now. The land seemed to want her, as well as him and Angela, and that was all right.

He heard Kallyn calling Devron and turned to find himself in the old barn outside the Gatekeeper's village. The fly-things' nest had gone but Tim was uneasy. Someone was trapped somewhere. He didn't know if it was Devron in trouble, or Hamett, or one of the Wardens. He didn't know whether they were in this barn or someplace else.

He was about to set off to help but he was back on the hill, with the warm sun and gentle breeze, and with Devron and the others still talking together.

The Gatekeeper rose and ambled over to him. *You've come to us twice when we've needed you,* he said in Tim's head. *You would take a great risk if you returned. Think carefully before deciding.* Then, aloud, he said, 'There's so much to teach you, Timoth. One day we could–'

Tim woke up. For a moment he wondered if he was at home or in Challenrah, then he realised he was still at Angela's house. Jasper was snoring softly, curled on a blanket beside the bed. What had Devron said? What had he been going to say that they could do? Tim tried to recall the Gatekeeper's words but the dream was fading fast from his memory. All he could remember was the sense of contentment at being in Challenrah, and at seeing the land restored to health.

It was a strange feeling, to belong both here and in Challenrah – two worlds so different and yet each with people he cared about deeply. How long would it be, he wondered, before he could go back to Challenrah? Would a Gate appear within days or weeks, or would he have to wait for many months? Would a Gate appear at all? The High Justice had said he was welcome to come back if a Gate allowed it. No, she'd said if and *when* a Gate allowed him to do so. Of course a Gate would appear – someday.

'Don't let it be too long,' he murmured. 'Please, don't let it be too long.'

He turned over and went back to sleep.

~ The End ~

Have you read the first *Timothy's Gate* book?

A magical, hidden world

just for you,

just when you need it

What could go wrong?

Read all about The Grey Lady, the shadowy raffakins, and how Timothy first discovered the magical land of Challenrah.

Timothy's Gate

by Sue Hoffmann

artwork by Katy Jones

UK £8.99

ISBN 9781910841501

Circaidy Gregory Press

If you have enjoyed the *Timothy's Gate* stories, look out for
Sue Hoffmann's *High King*

Imagine you are the first to set foot in a new land.

Keep imagining…

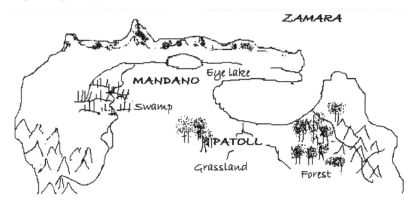

As the old country breaks down, ravaged by earthquakes and plague, an advance fleet of Almari ships sets out in search of the mythical paradise island that some believe awaits them far across the sea. They find a wonderful land, but a land with voices in the night and many mysteries to solve. And what has bcome of High King Lantor? When more ships are finally seen on the horizon, do they bring the old powers with them – or plague, disaster and new enemies? Young Zenton and his cousin are finding their strengths and becoming the leaders of their generation but what will they do when dissent and violence break out in paradise?

It should have been a sanctuary
　　　　– the refuge promised in legend

The Almari should have been safe here.

High King is an insightful fantasy, a rites of passage novel set in a land of danger, mystery and challenge.

Circaidy Gregory Press ISBN 9781906451805